99p

When t

SHIRLEY BOJÉ

HEINEMANN HEARTBEATS

Heinemann International Literature and Textbooks
a division of Heinemann Educational Books Ltd
Halley Court, Jordan Hill, Oxford OX2 8EJ

Heinemann Educational Books Inc
361 Hanover Street, Portsmouth, New Hampshire, 03801, USA

Heinemann Educational Books (Nigeria) Ltd
PMB 5205, Ibadan
Heinemann Educational Boleswa
PO Box 10103, Village Post Office, Gaborone, Botswana

LONDON   EDINBURGH   PARIS   MADRID
ATHENS   BOLOGNA   MELBOURNE   SYDNEY
AUCKLAND   SINGAPORE   TOKYO

First published by Heinemann International
Literature and Textbooks in 1993

Cover illustration by Kevin Jones
Cover and text design by Threefold Design

British Library Cataloguing in Publication Data
A catalogue record for this book is available from the British Library.

ISBN 0435 934 287

Phottypeset by
Cambridge Composing (UK) Ltd, Cambridge
Printed and bound in Great Britain
by Cox & Wyman Ltd, Reading, Berkshire

93   94   95   10   9   8   7   6   5   4   3   2   1

Contents

To the True Spirit of Africa –
the Source of which is Hope
and Peace for all her children.

1

Never Say Goodbye

A full African moon shone down on a man and a girl lying in a field. Wrapped in their love, they did not feel its silvery touch until Lindidwe shivered and reached for her jacket.

'Leave it,' said Sipho, pulling her back into his arms. 'I'll keep you warm.'

'No, Sipho, let me go.' Lindidwe slipped out of his close embrace and sat up.

'How can you whisper your love and then forget so quickly?' Sipho asked, hurt that she had pushed him away. 'Your heart cools quickly, *sthandwa*, and it's all because of your aunt. From the day she went back to the city, you've been different.'

Lindidwe heard the hurt in his voice and was sorry. She kneeled down next to him and cradled his head in her arms. 'I love you Sipho,' she said softly. 'I have loved you since I was a child and now you know me too well.'

Suddenly it was Sipho who felt cold. His Lindi was about to tell him something he did not want to hear. He pulled her hard against him. 'What is it?' he urged. 'Tell me what is wrong.'

Lindidwe pushed him away, her hands against his chest. He let her go, reluctantly. She was a beautiful girl. Her belly was smooth and flat; her thighs and hips slim and narrow and her breasts full and round. He loved her very much and wanted to make her the mother of his children.

'Sipho?' She turned to him. The moon polished her skin to the colour of new honey, casting deep shadows under her high cheekbones. He waited, his heart beating fast.

'I'm going away,' she said quickly. A cloud passed over the face of the moon and Sipho felt a shaft of fear and pain pierce his heart. It was a bad omen.

'Sipho?'

'I heard you,' he said gruffly and waited for the cloud to go.

'Then speak to me.'

But words did not come easily to Sipho Sosibo. A gentle, bearded giant, his speech came more slowly than his thoughts.

'Are you angry?'

He did not reply. Instead he stood up and began to limp away. Lindi felt his pain. Not the pain of the accident that had killed his father and shortened his right leg, but the pain in his heart. She knew how much he loved her and how much her words had hurt him.

'Sipho?' She went after him and he turned and caught her. His hand forced her head backwards and he bent his face close to hers. 'Why?' The word escaped from his lips like the cry of a child. Lindi's beautiful doe-like eyes flashed in the moonlight. 'Because I want to!' she cried and tried to twist out of his arms. But Sipho only tightened his grip. 'Why?' he demanded, the hurt turning to anger.

'Because I'm eighteen years old and too young to think of marriage and babies and things like that!' she cried, beating her small fists against his bare chest. 'I want more than that from life before I become a mother and a wife.'

Sipho laughed and let her go. 'If all you want is to see the world outside the village then I'll go with you.'

'No!' Lindi said sharply. 'I must go alone.'

She did not see his eyes suddenly narrow and his lips press into a thin line but she heard the change in his voice when he said, 'You don't want me around to spoil things for you. I see that now. You might meet some flashy new boyfriend who drives a smart car and lives in one of those fancy houses with high walls and iron gates. Is that it? Is it riches you want, Lindidwe?'

His full use of her name and his controlled anger were not

like the Sipho she knew. All at once she felt ashamed. 'You know that isn't true . . . it's just that my aunt only invited me and her house is very small . . .'

'So! This is not your idea! It's your aunt who has put this mad plan into your head!'

'And my mother and father!'

It was as if she had hit him. As tightly as he had held her, he now pushed her away. How could her parents agree to send her to a city where there was evil and death everywhere on the streets? He stared at her in disbelief.

'Sipho . . . don't be angry. You know that I love you and that I'll come back.' She looked at him with pity and hoped he would understand. She did not want to hurt him. He was so gentle and good. Even with a limp, he stood head and shoulders above other men; her strong, handsome lover with his short, thick beard and deepset eyes. He would be a good husband and father. But Sipho was happy to stay at Kwamakutha and be a trader and farmer. His love for the land and the wide clear sky was as great as his love for his sheep, goats and cattle. Nor was he a poor man. He made good money buying and selling livestock and running the small trading store his father had left him. Now that it was his, he wanted to make it bigger and better for Lindi and the sons and daughters that would be born to them. She knew this but from her heart, she begged him to understand the need for her to be free for a time. To see and taste life – the big, bright life of a city filled with excitement and adventure.

When Sipho spoke again his words were still cold. 'Even if you do come back, nothing will be the same again. The city will change you and I don't know if I'll like the change.' When she said nothing, he asked sharply, 'What does Old Granny say?'

Lindi shook her head. 'I don't want her to know.'

'Ha!' Sipho laughed shortly. 'A *sangoma* knows everything.

You know you can't go to a strange place without speaking to her.'

'Nothing she says will change things.'

'How can you be sure? Are you afraid of what the bones will say?'

'It is what my aunt says . . .'

'I don't want to know what your aunt says.' Suddenly Sipho changed his tone and took her hands in his. 'Please *sthandwa*, if you love me, say you'll go with me to see Old Granny.'

Lindi heard the plea in his voice. 'If it will make you happy,' she agreed and put her arms around his neck, pressing her slim body against his. But before he could kiss her, she slipped away and with the grace of a young doe, ran into the pale moonlit night, back to the home where she had been born and lived all her life.

———— ❤ ————

Sipho could not sleep. He lay awake, thinking of Lindi's words, words that cut deeper and deeper into his heart until the pain became too hard to bear. He had to stop her. If Old Granny did not do so, he would. He twisted and turned on his hard mattress, longing to hold her, to feel her soft girlish body pressing against his. Lindi! *Sthandwa!* Love of my life! Then suddenly the answer to his troubled thoughts came to him. If Old Granny gave Lindi her blessing to go, then he would make quite sure that she would soon be back. He would have to be sure that if things went wrong, she would blame herself and not him. But there was not much time. For his plan to work, Lindi would have to see the *sangoma* soon. Just before the first rooster rose to flap its wings and wake the villagers, Sipho fell asleep. His plans were made and only time would decide whether they would succeed or fail.

———— ❤ ————

'He wants me to see the *sangoma*,' Lindi told her friend Tombi Latha next day.

Tombi laughed. 'Your man is not like the others.'

'I know. Sipho is different and that's why I love him. Aiee . . . you're hurting me!'

'I'm sorry.' Tombi drew the comb more gently through Lindi's short, thick curls. The girls had tried a new hair wash Lindi's aunt had brought from the city. It was supposed to straighten their hair but also needed much pulling and combing. 'Well? Are you going to see Old Granny?'

Lindi frowned. 'She will throw bones and maybe tell me something bad.'

'Do you believe the bones?' The comb stuck and Tombi tried to keep Lindi's head still while she tugged it free.

'Sipho does. That's why he wants me to go.' Lindi's frown deepened. Sipho was so old fashioned. He was only twenty-three years old but what was good for his grandparents was also good for him. He would not listen when other young men spoke of change. He was proud of his people and his land. He wanted Lindi to be the same and she would be some day, but the seed her aunt had planted in her heart had taken root. The city would be everything she had dreamed of.

'He loves you very much,' Tombi broke into her thoughts. 'It must be so wonderful to be alone with a big man like Sipho. He's so strong and handsome. I would give anything to have a boyfriend like him.'

Lindi said nothing. Tombi was not a pretty girl but she had no shame. She threw herself at any boy who came along. Even Sipho, who did not like her.

'Lindi? Have you and Sipho ever slept together?'

Lindi's face burned. Nobody knew how far their love had gone. It was a secret she would not share with anybody. Quickly she bent forward and picked up her plastic framed mirror. Turning her head from side to side, she patted her soft, springy curls with a cry of delight.

'I like this new hair stuff . . . it's really going to work. We're going to make the other girls so jealous they'll want to know what we did to make our hair so pretty, but we won't tell them will we?'

Tombi laughed. Lindi was getting out of a tricky question but sooner or later Tombi would find out the truth. She always did in one way or another.

———————— ♥ ————————

It was there by the river that Sipho found them. He frowned when he saw Tombi. He had to speak to Lindi alone. Tombi saw him first, slowly limping towards them along the river bank. 'It's good we did your hair first,' she laughed and grabbed the comb from Lindi's hand. 'Here comes the passion of your heart but he doesn't look very happy. Maybe he'll cheer up when he sees how beautiful you look now.'

Lindi turned and saw Sipho wave. She waved back. 'It's because I'm going away,' she said. 'Here Tombi, take all this stuff home. I think Sipho wants to see me alone.'

Tombi put the towels, combs, mirror, shampoo and lotion in a canvas bag and zipped it closed. She did not mind going. Lindi would tell her everything anyway. But unlike Sipho, she hoped that Lindi did not change her mind about leaving Kwamakutha for a time. Tombi knew she would never stand a chance of getting Sipho's attention while Lindi was around.

'I've spoken to your father and he said that they only agreed to let you go if you see Old Granny and get her blessing,' were Sipho's first words to Lindi. He sat on a rock, cold and accusing. 'You lied to me . . . why?' He had seen Lindi's new hairdo but saw it as a start to her life in the city and did not like it.

'Sipho! You come here with your face like a storm cloud and say nothing about my hair. Don't you like it this way?'

Lindi tossed her head and looked at him from under her long eyelashes, her lips full and pouting.

'It's not you,' Sipho replied sharply. 'Now why did you lie to me? You said your father and mother had agreed that you went to your aunt.'

'It's true. They did.'

'But you said nothing about them wanting you to go and see the *sangoma*.'

'No, because *you* did!'

'So?'

'So I agreed, didn't I?' Lindi heard the anger in Sipho's voice and she too, grew hot with anger. 'You should not have gone to my father!' she shouted. 'This is between you and me! I didn't say to him that I would or would not go but now because everybody keeps on and on about it, I'll go!'

Sipho got up and put his arm around her. 'Lindi . . . *sthandwa*. I don't want to fight with you, but the city is an evil place and I don't want anything bad to happen to you.'

'Nothing will happen.'

'You don't know that. Go to Old Granny and let the bones speak for you.' Sipho tried to draw her into his arms but she pulled away.

'I'll go! I'll go!'

'When?'

'I don't know . . . tomorrow . . . the next day . . . There's enough time and now I don't want to talk about it any more!'

Sipho was unhappy about the way Lindi was behaving. He knew she was afraid of what Old Granny would say. The bones never lied. If she changed her mind and did not go with him, he would have to follow the plan he had made. It was the only way. He tried once more to soften her anger by taking her into his arms. 'I'll say nothing more about it if you promise to go with me early tomorrow morning. We can go to Old Granny together.'

Lindi sighed and nodded. Then she let Sipho kiss her. His

arms were strong around her slim waist and his mouth hard and demanding. When he tickled her ear with his tongue she laughed. He loved to hear her laughter. It was a high, girlish sound that rippled like water running over the river rocks. He clasped her more tightly to him, then picked her up and carried her to the grassy river bank where he put her down and lay next to her.

'Say you'll always be mine, *sthandwa* . . .' his breath was hot and sweet against her ear. 'If you go away, you will change and I will have lost you forever.'

Lindi turned on her side and rolled on to him, stopping his words with her mouth. When her hands slipped under his shirt and flitted like butterflies over his skin, he groaned, and gripped her shoulders. She tried to push his hands away. 'Somebody will see us,' she began weakly, her body melting at his touch, but Sipho got to his knees and held out his hand. 'Then let's go deeper into the trees,' he said.

'I want to, but . . .' Her mouth was dry and her heart beat fast. She was sure Tombi would come back to spy on them. If her friend saw them disappear into the trees . . . the thought of Tombi watching them decided her. Quickly she jumped to her feet and pointed across the river bank. 'Look, Sipho! Over there!'

'What? Where?' He turned as quickly and in that moment Lindi laughed and skipped away. It was a joke they often played when they got too serious. But Sipho did not feel like laughing. He tried to smile but the hurt would not go away.

As he limped towards her and saw her beautiful young body outlined through the thin fabric of her dress, he knew that with or without Old Granny, he would have to carry out his plan and make sure his Lindi stayed his forever. His relief was so great that he reached out and pulled her roughly to him, scraping his beard against her cheek. 'You're a little she-cat and you're going to pay for this . . .' He laughed and rubbed her face even harder.

8

Tombi, on her way back to the river had good reason for secretly coming upon the two lovers. When she heard Lindi's shrieks, she gave a sly smile. If Lindi did not want to tell her, she would soon see for herself. She hurried her step only to find Lindi and Sipho tumbling playfully on the grass.

Disappointed, she called out, 'Stop fooling around you two! Lindi . . . your father wants to see you!'

They sat up panting with laughter and stared at Tombi who looked at them with envy. 'Your father said I was to call you. A man from the Post Office has come with a message for you. It's from your aunt.'

Sipho cursed and looked away as Lindi quickly got up and brushed bits of grass from her hair and clothes.

'I'm coming, Tombi. Sipho and I were on our way home anyway.' She turned and looked at him. 'Are you coming?'

Sipho's shoulders hunched forward and he made no reply as Lindi bent and kissed the top of his head. 'I'll see you later then. Come Tombi, let's go.'

In silence, the two girls walked back along the river bank, leaving Sipho alone with the weight of sorrow that was breaking his heart.

2

Sorrow and Evil

'Aieee . . . eee . . . yah!' A shriek, followed by short grunts, was more the sound of some half-crazed animal than a human being, Sipho thought, his skin prickling with fear. He looked wide-eyed at the panting creature who crouched and swayed in the half light of the cave.

'You come alone, *insiswe*,' she croaked and with a wild leap sprang in front of him, flicking a switch of monkey tails across his face. 'Where is the maid? The one whose heart beats with yours . . . whose touch burns your flesh like fire? Why is she not here?' Sipho did not reply. 'Your shame makes you silent . . . yes, you Sipho Sosibo! As big and brave as you are, you are brought trembling to your knees because of this beautiful young girl who plans to leave you.'

'I love her!' Sipho cried. 'She is my life!'

The old woman screeched with laughter and leaped and danced in front of the smoking fire. Her thin wrinkled body was covered with strips of animal hide, ostrich feathers and monkey tails. Her headdress, braided with wildebeest tail hairs, coloured beads and small, odd-shaped bones, swung crazily above her dark snapping eyes. Many years ago she had the lobes of her ears slit open so that the skin could stretch over round wooden blocks. 'And where is this maid? Is her fear greater than the wisdom of the bones?'

'Her fear is very great, Old Granny.'

'And so is yours, young man. But your fear is from your heart's love for the maid and Lindidwe's is from a troubled spirit that gives her no peace.' Chanting softly, the old *sangoma* sat cross legged in front of the fire. From inside a pocket of skin that covered her withered breasts, she pulled out a small bag.

10

'I will throw the bones, Sipho, but already a cold wind blows evil and trickery across the footpaths she will follow.'

Sipho groaned. Perhaps it would be better if the *sangoma* said no more, but she had already tipped the secret objects out of the bag on to the ground. For a long moment she stared at them, then with a loud cry, threw back her head chanting and moaning until she went into a trance. Sipho felt sweat break out at the sight of her. With hands like birds' claws cupped around the bones, her body started to shake. She swayed backwards and forwards . . . backwards . . . forwards, faster and faster until she was short of breath and started to pant and grunt. Big drops of sweat ran down her face and, just when it seemed all her strength had gone, she gave another loud cry and flung the bones on the ground.

As the objects scattered around the ring of fire, Sipho jumped back in fright. Her eyes glittering, the old woman stared at the pattern the bones had made.

'Ahhh . . . it is as I expected.' With a deep sigh Old Granny leaned back on her heels and closed her eyes. For a long moment she did not speak, then – 'A storm-cloud that covers the sun . . . great birds with hooked beaks and evil eyes hunting a dove trapped in a silver cage . . . passion and weeping . . . much weeping . . .' Suddenly the *sangoma's* eyes dulled and she shivered. She pulled the skins closer around her bent shoulders, scooped up the bones and put them back into the bag. 'It is enough.'

'But what does it mean?'

'It is not for you to know the fate that awaits the one whose path you cannot follow.'

'But if I warn her . . .'

'She will not believe you.'

'Then what about *imuti* . . . medicine so powerful that she will stay. I will pay you everything I have for such medicine.'

'There is no such *imuti* . . . what is written, is written. The bones do not lie.' She got shakily to her feet. 'Put more wood on the fire, *insiswe*. Then leave me. I am very tired.' She turned to go but before she disappeared further into the cave, she stopped. 'There is one more thing.' Sipho laid the bundle of dry twigs on the fire and looked up. 'When words are too far to reach the heart, then the drums must speak of love.' She knew he would not understand, so she went on. 'The drums have fallen silent because the young men laugh at the ways of their fathers. But drumbeats that come from the heart bind spirit with spirit like the stars that shine on two people in different places at one time.'

Sipho was silent. He stared into the flames that burned high and strong like his love for Lindi. The *sangoma* was right. If he did not feed the fire, it would die. When he looked up, Old Granny was gone. He put more wood on the fire, then limped slowly out of the cave to find Lindi.

————— ♥ —————

She was not at home. 'Lindidwe has gone to the sweet potato fields with her mother,' Lindi's father croaked. Petrus Loma had worked in an asbestos mine. Over the years asbestos dust had eaten into his lungs and now it was hard for him to breathe. A sick and weary man, he could not work and most of the time sat in the sun. It warmed him and eased the pain in his chest.

'When she comes back, tell her I want to see her. I'll be in the shop.' Sipho patted the old man's shoulder and limped off to the trading store his father had left him. When he and Lindi married, he would make it bigger and better so that even in times of drought it would always bring in money. He did not like to be in the shop. It closed him in. It was better on the land with his crops of maize, *madumbies* and sweet potatoes, or with his long-horned cattle, goats and sheep. He hoped that Lindi would not keep him waiting too long. But an hour later it was Tombi, not Lindi who came looking for him. She squeezed between the desk and the shelf next to it so that she had to press close to Sipho sitting on a chair at his desk. She had put on a lot of sweet smelling scent and Sipho pulled away in disgust.

'Where is Lindi? And stop pushing me!'

Tombi bent her lips close to his ear and whispered, 'She can't see you, so she sent me with a message.'

Sipho got up and backed away. 'What message? Tell me and go. I'm very busy.'

Tombi gave him a big smile and shook her head. 'It's not that kind of message.' She pulled out a folded envelope from inside her dress. 'I walked a long way to bring you this.'

'Then give it to me,' Sipho said crossly but Tombi jumped back when he tried to take it from her.

'I would like a reward for my trouble first,' she said with her head to one side, a wicked smile on her lips.

'Stop playing games, Tombi, and give me the letter.'

Quickly Tombi stuck the envelope back inside the top of her dress. 'Then come and get it, or . . . I'll let you have it for a kiss.'

Sipho wanted to hit her. 'Why Lindi is your friend, I don't know.' He grabbed her arm and twisted it. 'Give me the letter and get out!'

Tombi's smile turned to a cry of pain. She jerked the letter from her dress and threw it on the floor.

'Take your stupid letter!' she shouted. 'I know what it says anyway, but when you get tired of waiting for your Lindi, you'll soon come and scratch on my window at night!' She ran off before he could reply.

Sipho cursed, then picked up the envelope and opened it. In pencil Lindi had written: *Dear Sipho . . . I love you with all my heart and I know you love me too, so please do not be cross with me because I am going away. Maybe I will not like the city and then I'll come back to you. I don't want us to fight so I think it's better that we do not see each other before I go. There will never be anybody I will love more than you. Please wait for me . . . your own true love, Lindi.*

Sipho crushed the letter in his hand and struck the desk with his fist. How could she tell him of her love and expect him not to see her one more time before she left? It was impossible to ask this of him. Even now his arms ached to hold her slim body against his. He thought of his plan to spend one more time alone with her. It would have to be tonight. If she loved him as much as she said she did, she could not say no. But there was to be no moon that night. By the end of the day, the sky was thick with clouds and the promise of rain.

Sipho limped home from the shop, angry and disappointed. He had to be alone with Lindi this one last time. He looked up at the sky. Perhaps it would not rain until much later. If they crossed the field and got as far as the woods near the river, they could shelter in thick bush. He would take a plastic cover and a blanket. He could not wait to see her and was glad that because of the clouds, the sky would get dark sooner than usual.

He ate very little that night and spoke even less. He could only think of Lindi. He wanted her more than he had ever wanted her before. At last, when he could not stand waiting anymore, he left his house and went to find her.

———— ♥ ————

'It's going to rain tonight.' Petrus coughed painfully. 'It's always worse when there is damp in the air.'

Lindi's mother, Nomsa, sighed and got up from the table. 'I'll put some Vicks in hot water. It always helps. Put the kettle on the stove, Lindi.'

Lindi did so, feeling unhappy about Sipho. She had not heard anything from him all day. Had Tombi given him the letter? She said she had but Lindi knew Tombi was jealous of their love and that Tombi would give anything to feel Sipho's strong arms around her. Maybe Tombi had lied about the letter.

14

Close to tears, Lindi turned from the stove and said, 'I think I will go to my room now, Mama . . . Baba . . .' She had no sooner crept into her bed when she heard a scratch on the window. Her heart jumped. Sipho? She listened for the sound to come again. When it did, it was harder and louder. She got up and pulled open the curtains.

'Sipho?'

'Yes, *sthandwa*. I must see you!'

'Did you get my letter?'

'Yes. That is why I have to see you.'

'But it's going to rain.'

'Not now. Not if we hurry.'

'I must tell Mama first . . . wait for me.'

Her heart beat very fast as she pulled her dress back on, said a few words to her mother, too busy fussing with her father to notice, and slipped barefoot into the arms of her lover. Sipho held her tightly, forcing her head back so that his mouth came down hard on hers. 'Never, never tell me that you love me but don't want to see me,' he breathed.

'I don't want you to be cross with me,' Lindi said between kisses. 'I don't want to go away with bad feelings between us.'

'Then come with me. I want to give you something that will leave us with only good feelings for each other.'

Lindi felt as weak as she always did in Sipho's arms. She knew this would be the last time they might be alone together and she was secretly afraid of the strength of their passion. At that same moment, Nomsa came outside, carrying a lamp.

'Lindi? Are you out there?'

The two lovers sprang apart as Lindi's mother came towards them, holding the lamp high.

'Wait! I'll be back!' Lindi ran forward before her mother could see Sipho. 'I'm here, Mama . . . what's wrong?'

'The Vicks is finished. If you are going to Sipho's house

ask his mother if she has some. Your father won't get any sleep if he can't breathe.'

'And if she hasn't got any?'

'Then Sipho must get some from his shop. The night is too long for your father to suffer. Hurry now, child!'

Sipho came out of the shadows and took Lindi's hand. 'Forget my mother . . . we'll go to the shop for the Vicks. It will soon rain and what better place to spend time alone together . . . come.' As fast as he could keep up with her, they went along the footpath to the store.

By the time they got there it was starting to rain softly. Sipho unlocked the door, helped her inside, then closed and locked it again. He put the lamp down then caught her roughly to him, at the same time kissing her hard. She struggled weakly but knew she wanted him as much as he wanted her. 'Come,' he whispered gruffly. 'We haven't got much time.' Tonight he would make his plan work. No more love games. If he could father a child by her, she would be his forever – even if the real act of love and fear of pregnancy did not stop her from going. Lindi tried to escape his urgent kisses, but they were hot and passionate. 'I never want to let you go!' he groaned. 'I've talked with Old Granny and the bones speak of evil things to come. Forget your mad plans to go away!'

'No!' Lindi kicked and struggled but Sipho would not let her go.

'Stop fighting me . . .' he begged. He ran hot kisses over face and neck, his hands bruising her flesh.

'Not like this! You're hurting me . . . Sipho stop! Please stop!' With all her strength she tried to push him away. He frightened her. Did love do this to a man? She loved Sipho as much as he loved her but something was wrong. The love they shared was sometimes wild, but always tender and caring. Not like this. When Sipho felt her tears against his mouth, his desire cooled. Lindi felt the change in him.

Sipho let her go, suddenly empty and ashamed. 'I'm sorry, *sthandwa* . . . I acted like a pig. It's just that I love you so much and I want to make you mine forever.'

Lindi crept closer to him and put her arms around his neck. 'I love you,' she whispered through her tears and kissed him gently. Sipho groaned and kissed her back.

The night was half gone when Lindi at last got home with the jar of Vicks. 'I'm sorry it took so long, Mama . . .' she began, but the house was quiet and her parents asleep. In the low burning light of the lamp, she saw a jar of Vicks next to her father's bed. Sipho's mother must have helped out.

She went to her room and lay on the bed. She could never doubt that Sipho loved her more than anything in the world. It was a love that, heartbeat for heartbeat, bound spirit with spirit and could surely never die. She listened to the soft drip-drop-drip of raindrops falling from the roof on to the water tank below. Like music of a love song, she thought and closed her eyes. She tried to match its musical beat with every drip-drop-drip an I-love-you . . . I . . . love . . . you . . . I . . . love . . . you and at last fell into a deep but troubled sleep.

3

Lost and Alone

Lindi stood on the platform of the big railway station, her brown cardboard suitcase next to her. She had expected to see the round, welcoming face of her aunt the moment she stepped off the train, but there was nobody to meet her.

She was alone and frightened. Was there some mistake about the day or time or place? She knew she was on the right station because the conductor had told her where to get off. Maybe her aunt did not see her because she was so different. She knew she looked smart and pretty in her new blue dress with her hair brushed softly around her face. Sipho had given her a gold bangle and gold hoop earrings as a going away present and the white leather shoes were a present from her father and mother. Did her aunt think she would come to the city looking like a poor country girl? But her aunt was nowhere to be seen. Lindi shivered. She was not cold, only afraid. 'Please . . . please auntie . . . you promised to meet me . . . please come.' What would happen if she did not come? She had her aunt's address but where would she begin to look? She did not have very much money and taxis were expensive. Crowds of people kept pressing around her. Everybody knew where they were going. Once or twice she thought she saw her aunt and sprang forward with a cry of joy, only to see surprise on the faces of the women who went on their way.

Above the noise of train sirens, whistles and loudspeakers, people shouted, and children cried. If someone called her name, she would never hear and she dared not move away. This was where her aunt had told her to wait and wait she would. She looked at the big round station clock on the platform wall. She had been waiting nearly an hour. She sat down on her suitcase, the knot inside her throat getting bigger all the time. She opened her bag and took out the paper with her aunt's address written on it, but it meant nothing to her.

Another hour passed. By this time it was late afternoon. Everybody was in a hurry. Lindi had never seen such madness in her life. It was as if a giant foot had struck an anthill, spilling out the ants. Still, they knew where their homes were and she did not. Where would she find shelter when it got dark? After another hour, she looked at the paper, now stained and crumpled in her hand. She would have to spend every cent she had on a taxi but what if she did not have enough money?

The crowds were starting to thin out as the sun set lower and lower. She was not at all happy about two youths leaning against the wall, watching her. They wore tight blue jeans and shabby leather coats. One looked very evil. He wore dark glasses and a black hat and a heavy chain hung around his neck. Both were chewing gum and laughed every time she looked their way. What if they attacked her? She decided to move further along the wall. They followed, hands in their pockets, laughing at her fear. She walked faster. She was afraid to go too far from people and when she saw a take-away shop further down the platform, she decided to wait outside the door. It did not stop the youths.

The one with dark glasses came up to her and put his hand on her arm, his face close to hers. 'Your boyfriend let you down, baby?'

She jerked her arm away only to see his friend press against her from the other side. 'Hey doll . . . we been watching you. Man, you've been waiting a l-o-n-g time now. How come a beautiful doll like you's got nobody, huh?'

They were so close Lindi could smell the mint gum they were chewing. She backed away. 'Leave me alone,' she said, close to tears.

'Hey now, that ain't nice, doll. Seems like you got no friends . . .'

'Yeah . . . nobody but us . . .'

Lindi felt trapped and terribly afraid. She tried to duck into the shop but they gripped her arms, almost lifting her off the ground. She swung her head and tried to call for help but a hand came over her mouth. 'That ain't nice, baby doll . . . you going to make Luke here real mad at you and when Lukey boy gets mad, he gets real mad . . .'

'Let me go!' Lindi struggled to free herself, tears spilling down her cheeks. 'Don't hurt me!'

'We ain't gonna hurt you, baby . . . we jus' want you to come along real easy now . . .' The one with the glasses picked up her case.

'No!' Lindi shouted then gasped, her eyes wide with fear as she felt the point of something sharp against her ribs.

'You be quiet or you get hurt, okay?'

Terrified, Lindi nodded. She could not believe that this was happening to her and nobody seemed to notice or care that she was in trouble. 'I'll give you all the money I have,' she cried, 'but please let me go!' She tried to struggle but the knife dug deeper into her side.

'You heard the girl! Leave her alone!' The voice behind them cut like a whiplash and the youth with the knife swung round.

'I said leave the girl!' Lindi could not see who it was but to her relief and surprise, she was suddenly free. She turned quickly enough to see a gun disappear into the coat pocket of the man who had come to her rescue as the two youths ran off.

'Are you all right?' The stranger came up to her. 'Did they hurt you?'

Lindi shook her head but the shock of what she had been through made her cry like a baby. Things like this did not happen at Kwamakutha.

'Here, take this.' The stranger held out a clean white handkerchief. He looked at her cheap cardboard suitcase. 'Are you alone?'

Again Lindi nodded. 'Yes. My aunt was supposed to meet me when I got off the train but she didn't come. I've been waiting since three o'clock.'

'That's nearly three hours. Do you know where your aunt lives?'

Lindi gave him the piece of paper. 'Do you know where this place is?'

The stranger nodded. 'Yes, but it's quite far away.'

'Too far to walk?'

He laughed. 'Much too far . . . and not safe for a young girl like you, especially in the dark. And a taxi will cost you a fortune. Forget it.'

'But what am I going to do?' Lindi's fear returned. This was a very bad start to a trip that should have been wonderful and exciting. Her aunt must have mixed up the date of her coming or else something had happened to her. 'I don't know what to do. I'm a stranger here . . .'

'Maybe I can help. What is your name?'

'Lindidwe Loma.'

'It's a nice name. Well, Lindidwe Loma, does your aunt have a telephone?'

Lindi shook her head. 'I don't think so.'

'Then this is what we'll do. My friend lives near here. Come with me to his house and we'll see if we can find your aunt. There are ways to find out if she has a 'phone. If we can't find her tonight, you can stay at the house and in the morning we can find this place where your aunt lives.'

Lindi shook her head. 'I don't know you,' she said quickly. He looked kind but good girls did not go with strange men, especially if they were taking them home. She knew her parents would not be pleased.

'Stay then, but I must warn you . . . the city crawls with

people like those two thugs who messed you around. A young girl alone in a city at night is asking for trouble. You can get beaten up or raped or your things stolen. Maybe all three things at one time and if you're not so lucky, they may even kill you. Life to them is cheap.'

'But the police . . .'

'Forget it! The police have their hands full. Women are beaten up and raped every day.' He saw that he had scared Lindi enough for her to change her mind.

'Look, if it makes you feel better, my name is Patrick and my friend is Richard Zondi. He lives with his . . . sisters, so you won't be alone. They are good people and will be happy to help you.' He picked up her suitcase. 'My car is parked on the other side of the station. Come with me.'

It was getting dark fast. There were not many people around and Patrick was right. She did not like the look of some of the men who hung around doing nothing. Unprotected and innocent, she had no choice but to go with him. Surely she could trust someone so friendly and kind, especially if he would help find her aunt the next day. These thoughts went round and round in her head as she walked with him to his car. It was a smart car and she said so.

'Not as smart as my friend's,' he laughed. 'He's very rich.'

As they drove through the city streets, Lindi stared wide-eyed around her. Bright coloured lights were flashing on and off, on and off from everywhere. Shops, bigger than any she had ever seen stood row upon row alongside the streets. Behind wide glass windows, silver white lights shone on to dolls as big as people, wearing beautiful dresses. There were all kinds of shoes stacked high and low on silver stands and jewels and more clothes. The street lights too, flashed beautiful colours of red, green and yellow.

'Pretty, isn't it?' Patrick looked at her when he braked at a red traffic light.

'It's beautiful. Everything is so big . . . so rich. Nothing like what we have at home.'

'You must see inside the shops. It's even better.'

'That would be wonderful. Perhaps my aunt will show me.' She did not see the strange way his lips curled when she said that or the way his eyes narrowed. She was too busy looking at the tall buildings, many with walls made more of glass than brick and clay.

Twenty minutes later, Patrick turned the car into a driveway off the street and Lindi saw they were now in a part of Bethsada where people lived. The houses were all different – some big, some small. Some had walls and others had wire fences. Richard Zondi had a high brick wall around his house with big iron gates.

'I can open the gates,' Lindi said but Patrick stopped her, saying, 'They open by themselves.' He did something outside the car window and to her great surprise, the gates did swing open by themselves.

The house was built of the same bricks as the walls and to Lindi, it looked as big as a hotel. Patrick stopped the car behind two other cars in the driveway. He was right. They were smarter and bigger. With such a house and cars, this Richard Zondi had to be a very rich and important man.

'Richard's car is here, so he must be home,' Patrick broke into her thoughts. 'Come and meet him.' He opened the door for her and she got out.

Lindi followed him down some stone steps and along a paved footpath bordered with roses and other flowering plants. The garden was not flat but laid out at different levels which she later learned were called terraces. On the bottom terrace was a big pond with a splashing fountain. When they got to the door it was open. Patrick went inside and called loudly, 'Richard? Ri – chard?'

'Not so loud, friend. I'm not deaf!'

Patrick and Lindi swung round and there in the doorway

Lindi saw a man looking at her with dark glowing eyes that seemed to burn right through her.

'Richard, this is Lindi. Lindi, this is my friend Richard Zondi.'

She stared at him, her mouth dry, her heart beating wildly. He took her hand and her knees turned weak as water. He was the most handsome man she had ever seen and he was to change her life in such a way that she would never be the same again.

4

Moth to a Flame

'. . . so there the poor kid was. Nobody to meet her, no place to go and very little money to get by with.'

Patrick and Richard looked at each other in a way Lindi thought was kindly concern.

'I'm very glad Patrick brought you here,' said Richard. 'I will of course help you find your aunt but now it's late and you must be tired . . . and hungry too. I'll get Beauty to make you some food and then take you to a room. In the morning we'll look for your aunt's house.'

'You are very kind, but I can pay you something for staying here.'

Richard laughed. 'Pay me? Maybe with something else, but not money.' He looked at Patrick and winked. 'Patrick has given me your aunt's address and I'll try now to find out if she has a telephone number. But first, come and meet Beauty. She'll take good care of you.'

'Beauty is Richard's sister,' Patrick said. Lindi saw Richard frown a moment then laugh.

'My . . . sister, of course. And Alyce. She lives here too.' Richard put his arm around Lindi's shoulders and led her into the hallway up some stairs to the top level of the house. His nearness made her feel dizzy. What was there about this man that made her feel this way? She had never felt like this with Sipho and Sipho was bigger and stronger. How far away he seemed right now. She tried to think of him in this big fancy house – his own words. She shivered. Whoever this man Richard Zondi was, she had to think of Sipho and only Sipho. After tomorrow, she would never see Richard again.

———— ♥ ————

Richard slapped Patrick on the back. 'You did well! This girl is perfect in every way! Looks . . . innocence and trust . . . like a child, she will believe everything she is told.'

'Maybe, but she didn't come easily.'

Richard laughed. 'Even after Luke and Danny messed her around?'

'That helped but it was only after she heard that worse could happen to her that she agreed to come with me.'

'And her family? Did she say?'

'Just this aunt who was supposed to meet her.'

'That is easy to take care of,' Richard said with a smile. 'After that, it won't be too hard to make her stay on with us.'

'How long before you can use her?'

'Not long. You leave it to me. You have done your part; now I will do mine. There is no girl who has not fallen for me. This one will be the same.'

———— ♥ ————

Beauty laughed. 'He said I was his sister?'

'Yes. Why do you laugh?'

'Listen kid . . . do I look like Richard's sister? Huh?'

Lindi's face burned. Beauty was lying on her bed dressed in a soft, shiny see-through robe that showed every curve and bump of her plump body. Her hair was braided with beads and hung to her shoulders and her round, puffy face was thick with make-up. A box of sweets lay on top of a magazine next to her.

'Fine! So I'm his sister and you are . . . yes, the innocent young girl lost in a crowd with nowhere to go.'

'That's true. How did you know?' Lindi stared wide-eyed at Beauty who got off the bed, draped the robe around her fleshy body and came up to Lindi. She put a fat, ringed finger under Lindi's chin and looked into her eyes. 'Then this strange kind man found you and brought you home with a promise to help?'

'Yes.'

Beauty sighed and turned away.

'Is something wrong with that?' Lindi asked with a worried frown.

Beauty shook her head and went back to the bed. She picked up the box. 'You like sweets? Here . . . take them. I should keep off sweets . . . too fat. You eat them, skinny kid.' She gave Lindi the box of sweets and made for the door. 'There's a room next to mine. You can sleep there. Alyce won't be using it tonight.'

'But . . .'

'Listen kid. I'm tired. I've had a busy day and who knows? I might have a busy night too. Somewhere in between I have to sleep.'

Lindi did not understand. How could Beauty be busy day and night? 'Are you a nurse?' she asked as she followed Beauty to the other room. Beauty stopped at the door with a shout of laughter.

'A nurse? Me? Kid . . . you've got a lot to learn and if you've come to the city to do that . . . you'll learn. A nurse? Wait till I tell that to Richard!' Still laughing, she shut the door after Lindi, leaving Lindi in a room full of riches and a lace and satin bed to sleep on.

———— ♥ ————

She was nearly asleep when she heard a knock on the door. She sat up. 'Who is that?' Nobody answered. She waited, staring at the door. The knock came again. She got out of bed, put on the silk robe Beauty had given her and went to the door.

'Lindi?' It was Richard with a glass in his hand. 'I've brought you a hot honey drink that will help you sleep well.' His dark eyes again seemed to burn through her clothes and she felt weak and shy because of the thin robe that covered her. When she took the glass his hand brushed hers so that she spilled some of the milk.

'Careful!' He wiped the milk stains from her hand with his fingers and his touch was like fire on her skin. Her heart beat thick and fast as she raised her eyes with a small word of thanks. It was still beating wildly after she had said good-night and closed the door. When at last she fell asleep, the man she dreamed of did not have a beard or a big healthy body. Nor were the arms that held her Sipho's. To her shame she woke up with the cry of another man's name on her lips. Richard! Was it possible that after today she would never see him again? She could not understand the sudden ache that came with the thought. It blotted out the picture of Sipho waiting for her back home. It blotted out her mother and father and her missing aunt. It blotted out everything except the need to see this man who had bewitched her and who made her feel weak and shaky at the very sound of his voice.

5

Can this be Real?

Lindi woke in fright. Someone was screaming. She sat up and put on the light. It was nearly dawn. Moments later the door burst open and Lindi was shocked to see a young woman fall heavily against the frame. Her clothes were torn and her hair tumbled wildly around her bruised and bleeding face. Sobbing with pain and fear, she pulled herself upright and saw Lindi staring at her. Half falling, half running, she went up to the bed and grabbing the satin sheets, pulled them to the floor shouting, 'Who are you? What are you doing in my bed? And you're wearing my robe! How dare you! You dirty little tramp! How dare you! Get out! Do you hear? Get out!'

She tried to hit Lindi, her arms swinging wildly but Lindi jumped out of the way. She was very glad to see Beauty hurry into the room and grab the mad woman's arms.

'Stop it! Stop it, Alyce!' Beauty held the woman fast. She saw the look of shock and horror in Lindi's eyes. 'It's okay kid,' she said. 'This happens all the time.'

'Slut! Dirty little . . .'

'Shut up, Alyce! You've said enough!'

'Who does she think she is . . . messing up my room!' she screamed. 'And what right does Richard have to put his little plaything in my bed?' She beat her fists against Beauty, shrieking and twisting like a mad animal. 'Let me go! Let me go, do you hear?'

Beauty slapped her hard and Alyce fell kicking and sobbing to the floor. Lindi pressed her hands to her mouth, her eyes wide with fright.

'Listen kid,' Beauty said. 'In the top drawer of the bedside table is a bottle of pills. Bring them.' Lindi was back in a flash. 'Two . . . give me two.' Lindi shook out two of the white tablets and gave them to Beauty. 'Okay, now water . . . in the bathroom through there . . .' When she got back with the water, Beauty lifted Alyce's head but the half crazed woman fought and struggled. 'Let me go! I'll kill you for this! I'll kill you . . .!' But Beauty was stronger and forced the pills between Alyce's teeth, spilling most of the water down Alyce's torn dress.

'She'll soon be okay. Here . . . help me put her on the bed.' They lifted the drugged woman on to the bed and Beauty covered her with a sheet. 'She'll sleep for hours and remember nothing when she wakes up . . . except the scratches on her face.'

'Shouldn't you do something about them now?' Lindi asked with a frown. 'She's hurt quite badly. What happened, do you think?'

Beauty sighed. 'She got beaten up again.'

'Here? In this house?' Lindi was suddenly afraid. 'Who would do this to her . . . and why?'

'Listen kid, in our kind of work it happens a lot.'

'But what kind of work is so dangerous?'

'Dangerous?' Beauty looked surprised.

'Yes. I thought I'd be safe here but now I don't know any more. I'm scared.'

Beauty patted Lindi's arm. 'It's safe enough, don't worry. Alyce was with a . . . customer and he got a bit rough with her, that's all.'

'But what did she do to make him so cross?'

'Kid . . . what you don't know you'll find out soon enough. Go back to bed and forget all about this.'

'I don't think I'll sleep again. I'll wait until Richard gets up.'

Beauty sniffed loudly. 'You'll have a long wait. Richard works most nights and sleeps most of the morning. Sure you won't change your mind?' She swept her hand towards the bed.

'What? Sleep here with Alyce?' Lindi was shocked.

'Why not? Bed's big enough and Alyce won't move for hours.'

Lindi shook her head. 'I'll rather wait downstairs.'

'Okay, if that's what you want.' Beauty yawned widely. 'Me? I'm going back to bed.'

Lindi followed her out of the room. The house was very quiet. Beauty had to be right about Richard working otherwise he would have heard all the noise and done something about it. What strange jobs these people in the city had. Some worked at night and others had jobs that got them beaten up.

She went into the dimly lit lounge and sat down on one of the big velvet chairs. She drew her legs up under her chin and put her head against a cushion. She had told Beauty she was not sleepy but it wasn't true. She could hardly keep her eyes open. What a terrible thing to happen to Alyce. What would Richard say? Nothing was real. Perhaps if she slept a little she would wake up and find everything a dream and she was back in her native village lying with Sipho down by the river. She closed her eyes and thought about him until she felt herself slipping into a dark mist of sleep. He had looked so sad when she had kissed him goodbye. Poor Sipho. She felt sorry for him but if he only knew the adventures she was having after only one day in the city. In her dream world she tried to tell him but he would not listen. She felt his arms go around her and then he picked her up. She moaned with pleasure at his touch and curled her arms around his neck, pressing small wet kisses against his throat. When he put her down on a bed of grass, she whispered, 'Don't let me go. Hold me and tell me how much you love me . . .' She reached up and pulled his head down so that his lips were close to hers. Instead, he kissed her cheek and

covered her with something warm. 'Sleep now . . . sleep
. . .' She frowned a little.

Something was different about his face. . . no beard . . .
Everything was so misty and unclear and her body felt so
tired and heavy . . . so very, very heavy . . .

———— ♥ ————

'Lindi! Lindi wake up!' Beauty pulled open the curtains and
bright sunshine melted away the sweet, romantic dream in a
flash. She opened her eyes and to her surprise found she was
in another room.

'How did I get here? I never . . . did you put me here?'
Her eyes wide, she looked at Beauty who set a mug of coffee
on the table next to the bed.

'Me? What do you mean?'

'I mean here . . . I never came here . . . I went to the
lounge and sat in a chair and I think I went to sleep . . .' She
frowned and tried hard to think what happened next.

'You've been dreaming, kid. This is where you've been
sleeping and where Richard said I'd find you.'

'Yes . . . I remember now. I was dreaming about Sipho
and then . . .' Lindi suddenly stopped and with a cry pressed
her hand to her cheeks. 'Richard? Richard said you'd find me
here?'

Beauty's round shoulders lifted in a shrug. 'That's what he
said. Now drink your coffee. Richard has news for you and
said you could go down to his study as soon as you are
ready.'

Beauty pulled the same white see-through robe around her
plump body and went to the door. Lindi looked away. It was
all too much for her. First that Beauty had no shame and
walked around showing her body for all to see and then the
terrible truth that the dream she had was no dream but had
really happened. Richard! It was Richard who had carried
her from the lounge chair to this room. Richard who had felt

her arms around his neck, her kisses . . . Lindi felt sick with shame. Her heartbeat quickened, sending hot blood rushing to her face. How was she going to face him again? Something like this had never happened to her before. She was not a heavy sleeper. She would have woken up if somebody had touched her. Was it the hot honey drink he had given her to make her sleep better? She tried to think. Why had it seemed so much like a dream? But to kiss him and touch his face! His face? She dimly remembered how smooth his skin had felt. She had wondered why at the time but she had been too sleepy to think straight. So it had not been a dream at all. Richard had found her in the lounge and carried her to this bed. What would she say to him? What would he think of her? Worse than anything, she had flamed with desire at the male hardness of his body. She tried hard to think what she might have said but could not remember. Then all at once her shame turned to anger. He had no right to do what he did!

She had to talk to him at once. She looked around for her dress and put it on hastily.

He should have made sure she was awake first – not just carry her off like that! She had truly believed him to be Sipho and she must have spoken his name. He could have done anything to her if she had believed him to be Sipho. How dared he make such a fool of her!

With each angry thought, Lindi grew more brave. Who did this Richard person think he was? It did not matter how rich or important or kind he was, he had some explaining to do. With a quick look in the mirror, she patted her hair, smoothed her dress and ran barefoot from the room. She had to see him before her anger cooled and her courage failed.

6

The Dream Fades

A strange man was sitting in a chair by the window and she heard angry voices through a closed door leading off the big lounge to Richard's office. Lindi stopped in surprise. She was about to turn and go when the stranger saw her in the doorway.

'You're new,' he said with a smile that pulled his wet fleshy lips over yellow, broken teeth. Lindi did not like the look of him. He was old and fat and his clothes were too tight for him. He looked at her with hot red eyes, his small fat fists squeezing and pressing a soft rubber ball. 'Come closer, girl. Come on . . . come on . . . let me take a good look at you.'

Lindi frowned and looked at the office door. She could hear Richard's voice raised in anger. 'I don't think I should be here. I'll come back later,' she said and turned quickly to duck out the way she had come, but the fat old man was quicker. He flung his arms around her from behind.

'Not so fast, my beauty.' He laughed and Lindi smelled stale beer on his breath.

'Let me go!' She tried to struggle free but he held her more tightly.

'You like to play rough?' He laughed again. 'I like it. I like it good.' She felt his hands on her body and tried to scream but his hand came down over her mouth. The next moment he threw her to the floor and slapped her hard across the face.

Before she could cry out, he put his hand over her mouth again. He was no longer laughing. 'One more word out of you my wild beauty and you'll be sorry.' He was kneeling over her and she saw his shirt buttons pop open over his fat hairy belly. 'What's your name?'

'Lindidwe,' she choked as he took his hand away. He smiled wetly, his small red eyes looking her up and down. 'Young . . . wild and very beautiful. Yes . . . I must talk to Zondi about you, hey my pretty one?' He stroked her face.

Lindi kicked and struggled. 'Let me go!'

The next moment she heard Richard shout, 'Get away from her you yellow-bellied dog!' They had not heard the office door open. Richard leaped across the room and knocked the old man to the floor. 'She's not what you think, you stupid old fool! Get up and get out! All of you! Get out and don't show your faces until I say so! Go on! Get out!'

The two men who had followed Richard out of the office slunk away without a word and the older man went after them, cursing and rubbing his flabby, unshaved jaw.

Richard bent and helped Lindi get up. 'Did he hurt you?'

'Yes . . . no . . .' She started to cry. 'It's . . . I got a fright when he threw me down. I tried to stop him . . .' She wanted to be comforted the way Sipho always did when she was upset or something bad happened.

At that moment she missed him very much. The thought of his strong, gentle embrace made her tears fall faster. She closed her eyes and swayed a little. It was enough for Richard to pull her to his chest and clasp her round her waist. He smoothed back her hair. 'I'm sorry this had to happen. If that dog's offal had done anything to hurt you I'd have killed him. Come . . . let's go into my office. I have news for you from your aunt.'

'So soon?' Lindi sniffed back her tears.

'Yes, but first come and drink some hot tea. It will make you feel better and then we can talk.'

With his arm still around her waist, he led her into the office. Only later did she remember how her heart had quickened at his touch and to her shame, how much she had wanted to feel his mouth on hers before the magic moment had passed and they were once more two strangers apart.

———— ♥ ————

'Are you feeling better now?' Richard leaned back in his chair and smiled at her. Lindi nodded and put the empty cup in the saucer. She tried to smile back but the way he looked at her with his deep glowing eyes made her feel weak and uncomfortable. He was so different from Sipho. If they stood shoulder to shoulder, Sipho would stand taller and stronger in body and build. But it would be easy to tell who came from the country and who from the city.

Richard had the body of an athlete – slim and fine boned without any fat on his hard muscles. His face was clean shaven and perfectly shaped; his nose straight and narrow, his mouth full lipped but hard. Unlike Sipho who always wore jeans and a T-shirt, Richard dressed like a gentleman and wore an expensive gold watch and gold rings on his fingers. Only one thing was wrong. His smile, which came easily enough, never reached his eyes – deep, glowing eyes like coals that burned right through her. It was a feeling that excited as well as disturbed her.

'Lindi?' His voice, like deep velvet, broke into her thoughts. 'I know you have just been through a bad time and now the news I have is not good either.'

'About my aunt?'

'Yes.' Richard moved some papers around on his desk. 'We found out that she doesn't have a telephone so early this morning Patrick went to the address you gave him.'

'Was she there?'

'No. The house was locked. A woman living next door told him that your aunt had to go away suddenly.'

Lindi frowned. 'Did she say why?'

'Patrick says she thinks it had to do with a sick and dying relative.'

'Where is Patrick? I must talk to him.' Lindi jumped up, sick with worry and disappointment. She was also afraid. She knew she was now helpless and alone in a strange, big city.

'Patrick isn't here, and there's nothing more anybody can tell you. I'm sorry. Your aunt has gone and if she said where she was going or when she would be back, the neighbour can't remember. She is old and deaf. All she said was that somebody came to fetch your aunt and that she left in a hurry.'

'That is why she didn't come to meet me!' Lindi felt her stomach knot. 'What am I going to do?' She looked at Richard. 'I only have a little money. My father was going to send me my ticket home later. It will take days before I can get the money from him.' She tried to swallow the ache in her throat.

'Don't you know anybody else in Bethsada?' Richard asked.

Lindi shook her head. 'No.'

'Then stay here.'

'Here? With you?'

'Why not? We have more than one extra room. Stay until your aunt comes back. Why spoil your holiday and waste good money on the ticket here when you haven't seen or done anything yet?'

Lindi felt the blood rush to her face. Richard was right. But to stay in his home, alone with him? It was as if he read her thoughts.

'You won't be alone with me. Beauty and Alyce live here too. Your room will be next to Beauty's. You will be quite safe.'

'I . . . I don't know. It still doesn't seem right.'

'It's not your fault all this has happened. Why did you come to Bethsada? Was it just to visit your aunt?'

'No. I wanted to see what city life is like. I wanted to have some fun and adventure and see different and exciting things and people and places and . . . just everything!'

For a moment she forgot her aunt as she pictured herself doing a hundred different and exciting things. Things that never happened in Kwamakutha or ever would. Her beautiful slant eyes shone and she laughed. It was the same rippling, happy sound that Sipho loved to hear. It was the first time Richard saw her look so alive and beautiful. She would be perfect for him. He could not believe his luck. He had known so many girls, beautiful and young like Lindidwe, but life in the city soon made them wise and cunning. He could not keep them long. This girl from a country village would innocently help him in many of his crooked deals. Once he had enough money, he would leave the country and live in another part of the world, safe from his enemies. The lie about the aunt was worth it. He knew Lindi was attracted to him. It would not be hard to make her stay.

'You are a beautiful girl Lindi,' he said softly. 'Such beauty must be seen. There are many exciting things out here for a girl such as you. I can show you so much if you will let me. Things and places like expensive restaurants and night clubs . . . play houses . . . concert and music halls and movies . . . the casino . . . I could go on and on.'

Lindi laughed. 'It is like everything I dreamed about.' Then her laughter died and she frowned. 'But my father and mother would never agree.' She did not say that Sipho would be even more disgusted. She did not want Richard to know about Sipho.

'Then don't tell them.'

'But they will know . . . I can't lie to my parents.'

'Then tell them as much as you think you should. You don't have to lie. Tell them the truth.'

'About staying here? With you and your sisters?'

Richard tried not to smile. 'Think about it, Lindi. I'll take good care of you and see that nothing bad happens to you again. I'll kill the next man who tries to touch you!'

Lindi shivered. She wanted to ask him about Alyce but it suddenly did not seem important anymore. Richard would take care of her. He had a lot of money and it was true, she would live like a queen in this house. It was very exciting. A chance that would never come her way again. She thought of Sipho and a life with him. So different and dull. She was not ready for that.

One day she would go back to Kwamakutha and they would marry. She would live in Kwamakutha all her life and be a good wife and mother. What stories she would tell her grandchildren some day! Perhaps it was written that these things would happen, that this man Richard Zondi would enter her life. Why else did she feel this strange attraction for him? Why else did her heart beat so fast and her knees feel like water when he touched her or even stood close to her? Had their spirits once joined in another life? Suddenly she thought of Old Granny. Perhaps she should have gone to see the *sangoma* before she left Kwamakutha. Then she would have known what to do. Sipho had tried to tell her but she had stopped him and she was sorry now she had. Why had she been so afraid?

'Think about it, Lindi.' Richard broke into her thoughts. 'We'll talk some more later.'

He came close to her and gently pressed his hand on her shoulder. Her heart beat faster and as he left her, she already knew what her answer would be.

7

Kisses of Fire

Beauty said, 'Alyce wants to see you.'

'When?' Lindi was glad to see Beauty wearing a dress even if the neckline was very low.

'Now, I suppose.'

'Is she all right? Say now she . . .'

'Listen kid, you can go see her or do what you like. Me? I got to go.' Beauty slung her bag over her shoulder and took a quick look in the big mirror in the hallway. She wobbled along on high heels that clicked on the stone floor but got only as far as the front door when Richard stopped her.

'There's been a change of plan,' he said. 'Today you stay home.'

'But what about the money? Frank planned this for days. You can't . . .'

'Shut up!' Richard gave a warning sign that Lindi was listening. 'We'll talk later. Now get out of that dress and change into something decent. We have a guest, remember.' Beauty's full lip dropped. 'If the kid's staying, how long do you think it'll be before she finds out what's going on here, huh?' Beauty gave Lindi a dirty look. It was all Lindi needed to make her change her plans. She felt she was not wanted. She left them together and went into the garden feeling unhappy and very alone.

Minutes later Richard joined her. Before he could say anything, she said, 'I don't think I'm welcome here. Beauty doesn't like me and Alyce will not feel any different.'

Richard laughed. 'Let me tell you that Beauty is jealous of you . . . and Alyce? You haven't even met her.'

'I have.'

Richard's eyes suddenly narrowed and he was no longer smiling. 'When . . . and where?'

Lindi told him what had happened the night before but like Beauty, he shrugged it off. 'It's the girl's fault,' he said. 'If she wants to mix with crazy people and get hurt, that's her problem. She's a big girl, Lindi. I can't play policeman over her life. Now, let's forget my two sisters and talk about you. What can I say to persuade you to stay?'

He lifted her chin and looked into her eyes but Lindi turned her head away. 'That's not all,' she said. 'You also made a fool of me. You should have woken me before you carried me off last night. I don't know why I didn't wake up but you shouldn't have let me believe you were somebody else.' She felt hot and uncomfortable. 'I thought . . .'

'What?' he asked softly. When she did not answer, he said, 'You thought I was your boyfriend because of what you said and did and you believed you were dreaming all the time.'

'Yes.'

'But it was no dream and now you feel I made a fool of you because I never stopped you?'

'How do you think I must feel? I can't even remember . . . I could have said anything!'

'You did.' Richard put his hands on her shoulders and made her look at him. 'Look at me, Lindi.' She turned her head away. 'Look into my eyes and tell me you are not attracted to me.'

'I . . . I'm not.'

'Yes, you are! You know you are! There is some magic between us. A spell cast by the spirits of our fathers perhaps . . . who can tell? But I feel it too!' His voice deepened and he bent and brushed her cheek with his lips. When he felt her tremble he came closer but she suddenly stiffened. She could not stop her heart from beating wildly but what she was allowing him to do was not right or fair to Sipho.

'No, Richard. I love somebody else.' She tried to pull away but still he would not let her go.

'Have you had his child?'

'No!'

'Then he has not paid your father for the marriage to take place?'

'No.'

'Then he has no proper claim on you!' He tried to take her into his arms.

'But he loves me and I love him.' Lindi said and struggled to be free.

'Lindi . . . Lindi . . . listen to me. You are too young and beautiful to be wasted in some low-down country village. You talk of love but you know nothing of it. I can awaken you and teach you things about love that no stupid village boy can.' He got no further. A red hot wave of anger came over Lindi and, before she could stop herself, she slapped him hard across the face.

She saw his eyes widen in surprise that turned to anger but as quickly it passed and he threw back his head and laughed.

'So . . . you are a little hell cat too!' He let her go. 'Now I suppose I must say I'm sorry and beg you to stay, but I won't. You will stay because you want to. Because no matter what you say, you like me more than you want to believe. It is your head that is telling you lies, not your heart.'

Before she could reply, he pulled her roughly against him and kissed her hard. Then he let her go and looked at his watch. 'Be ready to leave in fifteen minutes. I am taking you out to spend the most exciting day of your life.' Having said that he left her. How dare he, she thought pressing her fingers to her mouth. He was so sure of himself. So sure of her feelings for him. She loved Sipho. Only Sipho. Then why did he awaken feelings in her that Sipho never had and why was her heart beating with the desire to know him better?

Like a puppet whose strings were being pulled by an unseen and powerful hand, she went inside to change her clothes. It was only when she went upstairs to the bedroom that she remembered Alyce.

———— ♥ ————

'Beauty said you wanted to see me.'

Lindi stood in the doorway of Alyce's bedroom, ready to run if Alyce started screaming at her. But the thin, tired girl resting against the pillows said quietly, 'I can't remember if I shouted at you but if I did I'm sorry.' It was hard for her to talk through her cracked and swollen lips.

Lindi went into the room and stood at the foot of the bed. 'I'm also sorry . . . about your face and everything. It looks very sore.'

'I'll be all right. It's just my head. I can't remember things, you see . . .' Lindi saw tears in Alyce's eyes – eyes too big for her small, foxy face. 'That's why I have to warn you . . .'

'Warn me? About what?'

Alyce's tears fell faster. 'This house is evil . . . the people in it are evil . . .' She held out a thin hand to Lindi. 'Come closer . . .' Lindi frowned but moved forward. 'What's your name?'

'Lindi.'

'Listen to me, Lindi. You must leave this house . . . don't stay another minute. If you do you'll be sorry. You'll end up like me.' She took a deep, shaky breath then her eyes suddenly widened and she stared at the door, her hand to her throat.

Lindi turned around to see what had frightened her and saw Richard standing in the doorway.

'Here you are,' he said and walked into the room. 'You were supposed to get ready to go with me. I've been waiting for you.'

43

'Alyce wanted to see me,' Lindi said, still not sure why Alyce looked so frightened.

'Why?' He looked at Alyce. 'Is it so important that it can't wait?'

Alyce fell back against the pillows, her big frightened eyes on Richard. 'Yes, it can wait,' she whispered.

'Or maybe it can't. Since Lindi is here and we do have some spare time, why not finish what you were talking to her about? I suppose you wanted to tell Lindi about your bad dreams.' He looked at Lindi and pulled a face. 'Alyce always has these bad dreams. They are so real she believes them. Things like evil spirits coming into this house and scaring everybody. Next she'll tell you that all these pills she has to take help her to stop having these nightmares.'

'No! That's not true!' Alyce suddenly burst into tears and fell forward, her head to her knees. 'The pills help me remember things! I need them to keep me from going mad!' She started to cough, her fingers tearing at the sheets. Lindi saw her fall; her eyes rolling and saliva forming at the corners of her mouth. Richard grabbed her shoulders and forced her to lie still.

'What's the matter with her?' Lindi was shocked at the change in Alyce. 'Is she sick?'

'There's a bottle . . .'

'I know . . . in the drawer . . .' Lindi rushed to get the white pills but they were not there. To her surprise Richard had them in his coat pocket. 'It's a spare bottle. Can you get some water?' Lindi ran to the bathroom. Poor Alyce, to need pills so badly!

When Alyce saw the bottle of white pills, she tried to grab the bottle. 'Give them to me!' she screamed. 'They're mine! Mine! How dare you take them away! Give! Give!'

Lindi stared in shocked silence. Alyce was mad. Her eyes rolled and she was moaning as if in terrible pain. What sickness could make somebody act this way? Maybe Alyce had a devil in her. That is what Old Granny would say. People who had an evil spirit acted like this. Then the evil spirit had to be driven out and it was a terrible thing to see. White pills could never drive out an evil spirit. Only a *sangoma* could do that. Perhaps if she spoke to Alyce about it, Alyce could go and see a *sangoma*. When she had swallowed the pills, Alyce lay back and closed her eyes.

'Leave us now, Lindi,' Richard said. 'Get ready and wait outside for me. I won't be long.'

Lindi did so but halfway down the hall she thought she heard a muffled scream. When she heard nothing more she quickly went to the room Richard had given her. Maybe it was nothing. It was good that Richard was taking her out. She was suddenly ashamed of the cheap cotton dresses her mother had made her from material bought at Sipho's store. She would just have to wear her best dress and hope that Richard would not feel ashamed to take her out.

8

A Love Letter Lies

Dear Sipho. Lindi put down the pen. Dear Sipho what? I've met a man who is rich and important and much more handsome and exciting than you? Who thinks I am the most beautiful girl he has ever seen? A man who takes your place in my dreams? Who is showing me the fun and excitement of city life? All this because Auntie never came to meet me?

She could not write these things to him. What could she write that would make everything look all right? She could tell many lies but if the truth ever came out she would feel guilty and ashamed.

Dear Sipho, I don't know how to tell you this but my aunt never came to meet me at the station and a kind stranger has taken me into his house. No that did not sound good. She tore the paper and started again.

Dear Sipho, Please tell Mama and Baba that Auntie never came to meet me and now I'm living with somebody . . . No that was worse. What could she say? She bit the end of the pen and for a long time stared out the window. Then with a heavy sigh, she began again.

Dear Sipho, I am writing this letter to tell you that I am safe and well. When I got to the railway station, Auntie was not there to meet me. There has been a change of plan and I am staying with friends until Auntie gets back from looking after somebody who got sick and needs her. It was very sudden and I don't know everything but she will not be gone long. That is why I am waiting for her here at this friend's house.

Lindi frowned and tapped the pen against her teeth. It was not a lie and it was not the truth. *I am happy and these people are kind to me. I like Bethsada very much. There is a lot to do and see. Please write back to me at this address and tell me you are not cross because I did not go home. I will wait for your letter and will let you know what happens. I love you and think of you all the time. Your own Lindi.*

The last part of the letter was not true. She could not write the kind of love letter she knew Sipho expected. Things were different now. She got up and stood in front of the long wall mirror in her room. She smiled shyly as she looked at herself. She liked the new Lindi. Her hair, her clothes, the make-up. She threw herself down on the soft satin bedcover with a happy laugh. Maybe it was wrong to let Richard buy her so many things but he was rich and said that one day she could pay him back.

She closed her eyes. Richard was so wonderful and he had not tried to touch her again since the day she had slapped him. First she had to pay him back in some way for his kindness. Suddenly she had an idea. She jumped up and with a hop and a skip did a little dance, stopping in front of the mirror to spread her skirt and spin around on her toes. If only Sipho could see her now.

Richard's house was ten times bigger than the village houses. Her home was a square thatched building with two small bedrooms, a small kitchen, an even smaller bathroom and the biggest room was the family room. Nobody in the village had electricity or water that ran through pipes into their homes. It was a way of life in the country and only when city people came to visit did they know any differently. City people complained that life in the village was hard. Now Lindi could see why. Richard's house was like a palace.

Oh, the stories she would take back with her would be like something from a different world. And tonight she was going to go out to dinner and see her first movie with Richard. She would wear her new white silk dress and high heeled shoes and Alyce would make up her face and thread beads in her hair, if she was well enough. Poor sick Alyce. It made her think of the idea she had to help Alyce as well as herself. It was an offer Richard could not refuse. Singing a happy little song Mama had taught her as a small child, she skipped out of the room to look for him.

———— ♥ ————

'It's time the girl learned the truth.' Beauty's dark eyes flashed with anger. 'I am tired of playing this child's game with her. If she is to become one of us, we must tell her who we really are.'

'No!' Richard snapped. 'The girl is not ready to do her part. I need more time with her.'

'Maybe she is too innocent, my friend. She may bring us trouble, not stop it.'

'You're wrong. It's because of her innocence that she is perfect for the job.'

'Beauty is right,' Patrick said. 'We can't wait too long. Time is money and while this little plaything of yours is having fun and costing us money, time and money is running out.'

'Then send her home.'

Richard, Beauty and Patrick stared at Alyce in surprise. Alyce shrank back against the wall, her hand to her mouth, her eyes wide and frightened. 'She's a good girl. Don't do to her what you have done to me.'

Richard got up so quickly, his chair fell over. He stepped over it, grabbed Alyce's arm and slapped her twice across the face. She screamed and fell to the floor, her hands covering her face.

'You dare betray us by anything you say or do and you'll be sorry you were ever born, do you hear?'

Alyce cringed at his feet like a whipped dog. Without any feeling, Richard kicked her then went back to his desk.

Beauty laughed. 'Take away her little white dolls and see what happens then! She'll kill the girl for her white dolls, won't you Alyce?' Alyce moaned and started to cry.

'Get up,' Richard said sharply. 'We need your help because the girl likes you and that is important.'

Beauty sniffed loudly. 'Country slut! I don't like her. The sooner she gets the job done the better I'll like it.'

'Not so fast, my fat Beauty,' Richard said. 'When she is like clay in my hands she can get so good that we can use her over and over again.'

'The police will get her in the end.' Patrick yawned loudly. 'So why all this fuss? I say get her ready now. She's mad about you . . . any fool can see that. Get her into your bed and put more of the powder into her hot drink at night.'

'No!' Alyce cried. 'Not that! She's a good girl! Don't get her hooked.'

'It's the only way,' Patrick said and Beauty agreed. 'Between her longing for Richard and her mad need for the stuff she'll soon do what she is told.'

'As long as you don't get her need for the "fix" greater than the need for her to be careful when the exchange happens,' Richard warned. 'We've got to be very careful. If the police get her, we know nothing. It will be her word against mine.'

'Then when do you start with her?' Patrick asked.

'Tonight.' Richard got up and picked up the telephone. 'Beauty, tell Lindi to be ready by eight o'clock. Then leave me . . . all of you. I have to make an important call and after that I'll be out for the rest of the day.'

———————— ♥ ————————

Lindi was leaving her room to tell Richard about her idea when Beauty came in. 'Where are you going in such a big hurry?'

'I have to see Richard,' Lindi said quickly.

'He's out.' Beauty sat down on one of the chairs, her legs stretched out, her fat hands spread across her stomach.

'For how long?'

'All day.' Beauty saw the disappointment on Lindi's face. 'But he gave me a message for you.'

'What?'

Beauty saw the light come back into Lindi's eyes. 'He says you must be ready for him at eight o'clock tonight.'

'For the movie and dinner?'

'He didn't say.' Beauty shrugged and all at once saw the letter. She got up. 'What's this?' She looked at the loose pages lying on the table where Lindi had been writing to Sipho.

'It's a letter to my boyfriend. My parents can't read and I have to let them know where I am or they will worry.'

Beauty frowned and picked up the sheet of paper. 'You told him you are here? At this address?'

'Yes. What is wrong with that?'

Beauty was silent a moment then with a friendly change in her voice said, 'Nothing. If you like, I'll post it for you.'

'Are you going to the Post Office?'

'I pass it on my way to work. It's no trouble to post it for you.'

'You go to work at strange times,' Lindi said, folding the letter and putting it into an envelope. 'Why won't you tell me what kind of work it is?' She licked the flap of the envelope and closed it.

'I've told you. I serve customers.'

Lindi wrote Sipho's address on the envelope and gave it to Beauty. 'The same as Alyce?'

'Yes.' Beauty looked at the letter she would not post, but read later.

'Then if the work is so easy, maybe I can help. That is what I wanted to see Richard about . . .' But Beauty was already out the door.

'Later,' she called. 'If I don't hurry, I'll be late.'

Lindi sighed. She was glad that Sipho would soon get her letter. She hoped he would forgive her for not going home and for not having written sooner. But her date with Richard quickly put Sipho out of her head. Eight o'clock. She had her hair to wash and her nails to paint. She wanted to look very beautiful tonight. After dinner she would ask Richard to take her for a drive to see the bright coloured lights of Bethsada. They could drive to the top of the hill where they would be alone. This time she would not turn her head away when he kissed her. Trembling with excitement, she began to get ready.

9

The Deceiver

Night-time is a lonely time for lovers apart; a time when the mountains, valleys and plains throb with the beat of African drums long gone. When only ghostly sounds still travel through space as spirits of the dead whisper messages of hope and longing into hearts hungry for love.

Sipho Sosibo had no drum. He sat in a thick clump of trees listening to Lindi's laughter in the water that rippled over the river rocks. His hair and beard were wet with dew; his heart heavy from missing her, his arms aching to hold her. It was nearly two weeks and still no word from her. Why, *sthandwa*, why? The night wind caught his cry and carried it to the stars but the weight of his grief was too much for them. One broke away and fell from the sky to crush his heart. With a great sob, Sipho threw himself down and beat his fists on the soft, damp earth.

———— ♥ ————

A day's journey to the north, Lindi moaned with pleasure as Richard's mouth came down on hers. 'No . . . Richard, no.'

He laughed. 'Why is it that when a girl says no, she really means yes? Hey, *sthandwa*?'

Lindi's eyes snapped open. *Sthandwa*? Sipho's love name for her! 'No, Richard . . . stop!' But he only laughed the more. His touch was like fire but in the split second before her eyes closed once more, she saw it. A bright falling star that blazed a trail of tears across the sky.

———— ♥ ————

Lindi hugged Richard's pillow, wet with her tears. He had been kind and had brought her a glass of warm milk sweetened with honey, 'to make you sleep better' he had said, putting the glass in her hand. How could she tell him that milk made her sick – that if she drank it she would surely vomit later? But he had been so wonderful, so full of passion and tenderness that she did not want to hurt him and drank the milk. When she woke up an hour later shaking and sick, she found him gone.

She only just made it to the bathroom in time, glad that she was alone and would not wake him. Back in bed she tried to stay awake to wait for him but her eyes were heavy with sleep. As she drifted off, she remembered feeling the same that first night after she drank the hot honey drink he had so kindly made for her.

Lindi had no sooner fallen asleep than Richard had gone to find Beauty.

'Are you ready?' he asked shortly.

'Yes.'

'Then let's go.'

They left the house quietly, got into Richard's car and backed out, Richard putting the car's lights on only when they were in the street.

'It took longer than I thought,' Richard said as they drove through the quiet streets towards the city.

'And the girl?'

'Like I said, clay in my hands.'

Beauty laughed. 'Then why wait? Let's go for it baby, let's do it!'

Fifteen minutes later they went into a noisy room filled with tobacco smoke and the smell of beer and unwashed bodies.

Waitresses in glittering short skirts and skimpy bikini tops ducked away from the searching hands of men drunk with alcohol or high on drugs. Smiling and giggling through thickly painted lips, they carried trays of drinks from table to table.

In the centre of the room was a big square table and four chairs. Three of the chairs were already taken. The fourth, at the head, was empty. As Richard came to the table, the other three men stood up. Richard greeted them with a nod, then all four sat down. Beauty came forward and slammed a new pack of playing cards on the table. She leaned over Richard and said in his ear, 'When the game is halfway through, the Boss will be ready to see you.' Then she straightened and said loudly, 'Well boys? Can I cut and deal now?'

Her fat, ringed fingers flew over the pack of cards as she shuffled them over and over until she was satisfied that they were completely mixed. Then she slammed them down on the table again. 'Okay, everybody happy?'

In answer to their silent nods, she picked up the pack and her hands flashed swiftly round the table as she flipped the cards from player to player.

The game could go on well into the hour before dawn. Money bets were high and Richard almost always won the poker game. It was a sick and shaking group of players who usually left the gambling table, poor and broken men.

Two hours later, Beauty went up to Richard. She tapped him on his shoulder. 'Okay, boys. We settle now.' She looked at a man with a badly scarred face standing next to Richard. 'You know what to do Chip, so do it.' The man nodded and took Richard's place at the table. There was to be no cheating or fighting when it came to paying out the winner. Chip knew his job.

——————— ♥ ———————

'Is the girl ready?'
'I need more time.'

'A day? A week? A month? Why not a year?' the old man sneered. 'What's wrong with you, Richard? Losing your touch?'

'She's different, Boss. Girls from country villages don't easily lie or cheat or steal or do anything against the law.'

'You know what to do so get on with it.' The Boss sat back in his padded leather chair and smiled, showing broken, tobacco stained teeth. He was a big man with small pig eyes disappearing into the fat greasy folds of his flabby face.

His clothes and manner did not seem right on a man as rich as he was. He also ate and drank like a pig and the vests and pants he always wore were stained with food and drink. But the Boss was the most feared and respected man in the organisation. Death came quickly to those who got in his way. He looked at Richard and belched loudly. 'The Fun Fair will be closing down its show ten days from now. Have the girl ready by then.'

'Ten days?' Richard frowned. 'That's not enough time.'

'Ten days!' The Boss banged his fist on the desk and cursed. 'Now get out!'

Chip was waiting for Richard outside. In silence he gave Richard a thick brown envelope. Richard took it with a nod of thanks.

'Is Beauty ready to go?'

'I'm here.' Beauty joined them, looking somewhat the worse for wear.

———— ♥ ————

When Lindi opened her eyes to the start of a new day, Richard and Beauty were ending theirs. She would not see them till past noon. Unhappy, lonely and longing to tell Richard of her plan to fill the empty hours of the day, she hung around the house waiting for him to wake up. She tried to find Alyce but Alyce was also fast asleep, a bottle of spilled white tablets lying next to her bed.

It was nearly lunch hour when Beauty found her standing outside Richard's bedroom door.

'What do you think you're doing?' Beauty grabbed Lindi's arm, but Lindi shook her off. 'I want to see Richard. There's something I have to ask him.'

'What is it you want to ask him? It's about me, isn't it? You don't like me and you think because Richard . . .'

'It's not about you. It's about Alyce if you must know.'

'What about her?'

'I want to take her job until she's better.'

Beauty stared at her then laughed until tears ran down her cheeks. 'You? You want Alyce's job? Do you know how Alyce makes money?'

'She serves customers . . . you told me so.'

'You stupid, innocent fool! Listen to me, kid and listen good 'cos I'm going to tell you some facts of life that the sooner you know about the better for all of us, see? I'm sick of you hanging around here with your lovesick eyes and pretty little innocent ways. There's a tough world out there and it's time you got to know just how cruel and hard it is.'

Beauty's eyes glittered as she spat the words at Lindi and grabbing Lindi's arm, half dragged, half walked her to Alyce's room. 'There! Do you see that?' She pushed Lindi through the door and pointed a shaking finger at Alyce who was still asleep.

'Don't wake her . . . she's sick.' Lindi tried to free herself from Beauty's hard grip.

'Sick? You think that little slut's sick?'

Lindi looked at Alyce, afraid she might wake up, but Alyce did not move.

'She's not sick . . . she's drugged! She's so full of dope that when she comes round she'll last only so long . . .' Beauty snapped her fingers in disgust '. . . and she'll be slobbering for more. She'll do anything . . . anything to get her hands on what she calls her little white dolls. You know what I'm talking about kid?'

Lindi remembered the sweet and sickly smelling grass the old men used to smoke back home. A kind of grass that grew wild in the fields around Kwamakutha. The old men and sometimes even the old women smoked this grass. They said it made them happy. They could forget all their troubles and worries when such good feelings came over them. But the feelings did not last long and they would smoke more and more. In the end they became like Alyce.

Beauty saw her bottom lip tremble. 'So! You do know what I'm talking about?'

'Where does she get these terrible pills? Why do you let her have them?'

'She works for them, you fool! By selling her skinny little favours to anybody wanting to buy them!'

Lindi drew a quick breath and turned away from the bed.

'That's right, kid . . . she's nothing more than a dope addict and a whore!'

Lindi hid her face in her hands. 'I don't want to hear any more . . . get out of my way!'

She did not see Richard outside the door as she ran out and fell blindly against him as he caught her in his arms.

10

A Warning of Evil

'Why have you not been sleeping well, *sthandwa*?' Richard stroked Lindi's head, then kissed it gently. She put her hand over his mouth. 'Don't call me that,' she said and turned her head away.

It was more than three weeks since she had written to Sipho. She was hurt because he had not written back. Beauty said she had posted the letter the same day Lindi had written it. He would have got it long ago. There was also no more news from her aunt. Not that she really cared. She and Richard had become lovers and she liked living with him in his big, beautiful house. She had everything she wanted. Clothes, food unlike anything she had ever tasted, servants to cook and clean, the swimming pool, television and some-times a day or night out with Richard. He had taken her to movies and a music hall and they had eaten dinner at restaurants where she had learned to drink wine. It made her head light and dizzy but it was a good feeling because then it was easier to laugh, joke, flirt and make love.

'Take me out tonight, Richard. Some place special?'

'I have to work tonight.'

'You always work at night. Why?'

'It's the kind of work I do. Some people work in the day, I work at night.'

'Doing what? You've never told me how you make so much money.'

'Because it has nothing to do with you and if there is one thing I hate, it's a woman who nags or whines.' For the first time Lindi heard the anger in his voice – anger at her. It brought a sudden twist of pain to her breast and with it, a feeling of fear.

'I'm sorry.' She jumped up and threw her arms around his neck. 'I won't ask again.'

'Don't.' Richard unwound her arms and looked at her. 'And don't try to stay awake when I leave you. The honey and milk should put you to sleep like a baby. I don't understand why you have trouble sleeping.'

Lindi sat on the edge of the bed. 'Richard . . . don't be cross . . . It's . . . I can't drink milk . . . it makes me sick . . . ever since I was born.'

'So?'

'I . . . I've been pouring it into the toilet.'

She looked up and thought he was going to hit her.

'You what?!'

Lindi hung her head. It was their first fight and she was hating it. She suddenly felt naked and helpless before Richard's anger.

'Do you still love me?' Her eyes shone with tears and she tried to swallow the aching lump in her throat.

'You are such a child!' His handsome face twisted cruelly. He saw how crushed and unhappy she was and he liked the feeling of power it gave him. 'You should have told me. Why waste a good drink?'

His mind was working fast. All this time he thought he was getting her hooked on a drug he himself had put into the many glasses of milk and honey. What would the Boss say? Worse still, what would he do? He would have to try something else and it was time that Beauty and Alyce did their part too.

———— ♥ ————

Lindi picked up the pen and went on with her letter to Sipho. . . . *so because I have not heard from you, I thought I would write again. I have still not heard from Auntie but these people are very good to me and time passes quickly. There is so much to see and do* . . . She bit the end of the pen and stared at the sheet of paper. If only she could write about all the fun she was having and places she was going to, but Sipho would not like it and he had to read the letter to her parents. She sighed. There was not much more she could say except: *I will wait every day for your letter dear Sipho, so please write soon with all the news from home. Lindi.*

She sealed the letter and went downstairs to the office for a stamp. The office door was closed but she heard Richard's angry voice, then Alyce shouting and Beauty shouting even louder.

'Quiet! Do you want the kid to hear?'

Lindi backed away. This was about something she was not supposed to hear.

'I won't do it! I tell you. I won't do it!' Alyce was shouting.

'Yes, you will!' Richard said in a hard voice. 'Just remember how lonely you get without your little white dolls. So lonely you go mad without them . . .'

Alyce gave a loud cry and Lindi heard a chair overturn. Next moment she heard the sound of a hard slap and Alyce screamed. Lindi did not want to hear any more. Afraid of being found out, she turned and ran from the room. Whatever the fight was about, it had nothing to do with her. Alyce was always screaming or crying about something. Lindi did not feel so sorry for Alyce any more.

She put the letter on the hall table. She would get the stamp later. Without thinking more about the fight in the office, she went into the garden to wait for Richard. She had to know if he was still cross with her. The thought of losing his love over some stupid thing she had said was more than she could bear. In some way she had to make it up to him.

———— ♥ ————

She had waited no more than a few minutes when Alyce found her sitting on a bench under the shade of a mango tree.

'Lindi . . . I must talk to you!' Her face was still puffy and her eyes red from crying. She was shaking all over. 'Listen to me . . . you've got to get away! Leave . . . now! Before it's too late!' She sat down next to Lindi and shook her arm. She sounded breathless, her tongue flicking her lips. 'Richard is a bad man! More than that . . . he's evil! If you don't believe me then look at me . . . go on look!' She grabbed Lindi's arms and pushed her face close to Lindi's.

Lindi tried to push Alyce away. 'You're sick, Alyce. That's why you don't look good.'

'Sick? Yes, I'm sick because that evil man made me sick! And he's doing the same to you! I was like you! A fresh young girl from the country. I ran away from home. I wanted a job in the city but I knew nothing. There were no jobs. I had no money and nowhere to sleep. Richard found me on the streets . . . lonely and frightened and hungry. He brought me here and we became lovers. He got me to take hot drinks at night . . . drinks so full of dope that I soon could not live without them. He gave me more and more and then suddenly started taking them away. That was when I knew I was hooked! Do you hear me? Do you hear what I am saying?'

Lindi stared at Alyce who was crying and shaking with spasms she could not control.

'But you are his sister . . . he told me so.'

'He lies! Everything he tells you is a lie! He's a liar and a cheat and he is doping you too so that you will never leave this house . . . you'll be like clay in his hands. He'll use you . . . and break you . . . just like he did with me! You've got to believe me!'

'Enough, Alyce! You have said enough! Go to your room at once!'

Richard and Beauty had heard every word. Lindi ran up to him and he pulled her roughly to him, his arm around her shoulders. Alyce stood with her hands to her face, shaking and sobbing loudly.

61

'Take her inside,' Richard said to Beauty, then took Lindi in his arms. 'Are you all right?'

'She was telling me the most terrible lies about you,' Lindi said and looked up at him.

He bent and kissed her. 'My sweet, sweet Lindi. Forget about Alyce and think only of us. You wanted to do something special today and we will. Just the two of us together.'

He smiled over the top of her head as she clung to him. If his power over this girl was so great that she easily took his word against Alyce's he did not have to worry about adding any drugs to make her do whatever he asked.

11

Fun at the Fair

The Boss looked at Richard through the slits of his small pig eyes. His white cotton vest was stained with curry and beer. He belched loudly as he pushed the empty plate and bottle away. 'Well?' he asked shortly. 'Is she ready?'

'She's ready, Boss.'

'Good . . . good.' He rubbed his fat greasy hands together and reached for a cigar. 'Want one?' He pushed the box to Richard who took one and put it in his shirt pocket. 'You know the plan?'

'Yes.'

'And the rules?'

'Yes.'

'And if the girl fails . . .'

'She won't.'

'Good.'

'Then I'll see you in forty-eight hours.'

'With the bear.' The Boss blew out a thick cloud of cigar smoke. 'I can't wait to get my hands on that big old yellow bear, Rich!'

'As long as you remember that I like toy bears too.'

The Boss threw back his head and laughed loudly. 'For that you can take the whole box of cigars!'

Richard got up and with a nod of thanks for the gift, left the room, closing the door behind him.

------ ♥ ------

When Lindi came out of the bathroom wearing a short lace nightdress, Richard was waiting for her.

'You look like a princess,' he said. 'A beautiful young princess.'

'And you are my handsome prince,' she laughed as he pulled her against him. 'Aren't you going to work tonight?'

'No. Tonight I'm taking you to a Fun Fair. The show comes to an end tomorrow and I don't want you to miss it, so get dressed and let's go have some fun.'

'Now? Isn't it too late to go out?'

'No, the real fun only starts later. You'll see . . . you'll love it.'

'What do I have to wear to this . . . Funny Fair?'

Richard smiled. 'Anything you like . . . jeans and a shirt is fine. There's nothing fancy there.'

It was not long before they were on their way. At the Fair, coloured lights shone through a thin veil of dust kicked up by crowds of people moving in different directions.

There were clowns running around with whistles and balloons and side-shows with people shouting at the tops of their voices. There were donkey carts and pony rides; ice-cream and popcorn stands; sweet stalls, barbeques and hotdog stands. Lindi saw giant swings and pedal cars and big toy cars racing up and down on iron rails – so fast that the people in them screamed with fear and excitement. She had never seen so many people together in one place. Babies and children got lost and cried for their mothers. Men hooted and whistled at women and girls who shrieked with laughter. People walked about eating and drinking; empty cans, bottles, paper cups and bits of paper and plastic were dropped and trampled into the ground. She held on to Richard's arm trying not to bump into anybody or step on something a child was pulling or pushing.

'Don't lose me,' she said in his ear. 'I'll die if you do.'

Richard laughed. 'Come, I'll take you for a ride on a roller-coaster and then it's my turn at a side-show. I'll show you how good I am with a gun.'

'You're going to shoot somebody?' Lindi stopped and looked at him in shocked surprise.

'Not somebody . . . something.' He pulled her along to where people were buying tickets for a ride on the roller-coaster. 'Come on, don't be scared. You're in for the ride of your life!'

She was not very happy about the ride. People did not give terrified screams if they were having fun. They were getting out of the small open cars, shaking – some laughing, some crying.

'Come on . . . let's go.'

Before she could say anything, he had her inside the little car and was strapping her in. 'When it starts to move, hold on tight.'

Richard was right. It was a ride she would never forget. Not even her great-grandchildren would ever believe her – if she lived long enough to tell them. She was sure she was going to die. She screamed and screamed. Tears rolled down her cheeks but dried quickly with the wind that whipped her face and hair. It tore the words of fear and panic from her lips, spinning them into the sky. She felt she was falling to her death and only long afterwards did she remember that when her fear was greatest, she was calling Sipho's name, not Richard's. When the car at last came to a slow, smooth stop, she was sobbing loudly. Richard only laughed. 'It's just because it's the first time. Next time you'll love it.'

'Never! I'd rather die some other way!' She wanted to be sick and could not stop shaking. She could not walk properly and hung on to Richard's arm.

'I know what will put back a smile on your lips,' he said. 'See over there? That side-show? I'm going to win the biggest toy bear just for you.'

Lindi followed him silently to the stall. She was still too upset to notice Richard say a few quiet words to the man at the stall or see something pass between them before the man gave Richard a gun.

'See that yellow bear on the top row? The one next to the

rag doll with the string hair? I'm going to get it for you.' He lifted the gun, pointed it at some numbers moving in a circle in front of the toys. When he pulled the trigger, he hit a number which fell over.

'Ha! This is your lucky night, sir. Let me see . . . you have hit number twenty-four . . . a very lucky number. It means you can choose any of the toys on the top row.'

'The yellow bear . . . the big one on the right.'

Later, walking back to the car, Lindi did not know that the bear she was pressing to her breast had been chosen for her a long time ago. In less than a week it would bring her so much sorrow that she would carry the scars of her pain for as long as she lived.

12

All is Lost

'Richard, where is Alyce?'

It was early morning and they were still in bed. Lindi rolled on to her side and looked at Richard sitting up and drinking coffee. 'I haven't seen her since the day she said those terrible things about you.'

'She's not here.'

'I know that, but where has she gone?'

'She's in a hospital. It's better this way. She was getting very bad . . . even dangerous.'

'Did she want to go?'

Richard put down his cup and got up. 'We did what was best for Alyce. Now, no more questions. Where is the bear I gave you?'

'In my room.'

'Go get it.'

'Why?'

'Don't ask why – just do as I say.'

Lindi got up and went to get the bear.

'Give it to me.' Richard took the bear and turned it over and over. 'Lindi?' He put the bear on the bed and patted its head. 'There is something I want to ask you.'

'What?'

'You will think this very strange but . . .' He stopped and walked to the window and back before going on. 'It's about Alyce.'

'What about her?'

'I think I must tell you that Alyce is very sick. The doctors think she may even die.'

Lindi stared at him, her hand to her mouth. 'I didn't know she was so sick!'

'Nor did I. But that is not all.'

'What do you mean?'

'When I took Alyce to hospital, she screamed and put up an ugly fight. She didn't want to go and said terrible things to me. She also said she never wanted to see me again.'

'Your own sister said that?'

'That is what makes me so sad . . . and hurt.'

'What can I do to help?'

Richard sat on the edge of the bed and picked up the bear. 'When Alyce was a small child, a white girl gave her a bear like this one. They were friends because our mother worked for her mother. Then when they moved away, this girl gave Alyce the bear as a goodbye present. Alyce loved the bear very much. One day somebody stole it and she never saw it again. Now that her mind is like a child's, I want you to go and visit her in hospital and take this bear with you. Show it to her . . . let her keep it a few days. If she does not have long to live, this small thing you can do for her will make her very happy.'

'Why don't you take it to her?'

'She doesn't want to see me, remember? I don't want to upset her. It's still too soon.'

'So you want me to visit her? With the bear?'

Richard nodded. 'It will make me happy . . . and Alyce too.'

'When do you want to go?'

'Tomorrow.'

Lindi smiled and hugged the bear. 'I'll do anything for you, you know that.'

'Then how about a bigger hug for me?' He bent over and pulled her to him. 'My beautiful princess. How lucky I am to have found you.'

———— ♥ ————

In the middle of that night, Richard knocked on the door of the dim, smoke-filled gambling room.

'Come in!'

Richard opened the door. When the Boss saw who it was he slapped the behind of the half naked girl on his lap and pushed her to the floor. 'Get out baby . . . I got business to talk.' The girl looked at Richard with big frightened eyes, her hair falling over her face. Then with a small cry, she crawled out the door on her hands and knees, giving them both a last frightened look.

'Is everything ready?' The Boss spat tobacco juice on the floor and rubbed his hairy stomach with a fat, greasy hand.

'Everything is ready.'

'The time? The place? You have planned this carefully?'

'Yes.'

'Then tomorrow this time the bear will be with me?'

'Fat and full.'

'Good . . . good.' The Boss showed his broken yellow teeth in a smile that looked more like the snarl of an animal. 'I look forward to seeing my new furry friend . . . and Rich? When you go, tell Baby Doll I haven't finished with her.'

When Richard left the room, the girl saw him coming. He gave her a short nod and went back to the gambling den. Sick with fear and hate, the girl crawled back into the Boss's dirty, evil smelling den.

———————— ♥ ————————

The hospital was half an hour's drive away. Lindi sat next to Richard, the bear on her lap. She was not sure that Alyce would be happy to see her but she had always been a better friend to Lindi than Beauty.

When at last they drove through the hospital gates, Richard parked the car in the parking lot and said, 'Go through the entrance door over there . . . see it?' She nodded. 'Ask for Alyce Zondi. One of the nurses will take you to her.'

'And you'll wait here for me?'

'Yes. I'll be here.'

She got as far as the end of the parking lot when she heard running footsteps behind her. Somebody shouted and she turned to see what was wrong. At the same time, she was knocked to the ground and the bear was taken from her. She screamed for help and saw Richard run to her. 'I saw who it was! I'm going after him!' he shouted. 'Are you okay?'

'Yes . . . hurry! You'll lose him!' Lindi got to her feet shocked and afraid. Richard ran off and left her rubbing her grazed and bleeding arm. Minutes later she saw him coming back and with a cry of relief, saw he had the bear.

'You got it back!'

'Yes. The stupid fool wanted it for his daughter.' Lindi took the bear. 'What did you do to him?'

'Nothing. He was very sorry, crying and begging me not to call the police. He whined about how poor he was and his child was sick . . . the same old story you hear every day.'

'So you let him go?'

Richard shrugged. 'We got the bear back.'

'And now? Do you still want me to go to Alyce?'

'Yes . . . you'll be all right.'

'Are you sure?'

'Would I say yes, if I wasn't?' He bent and kissed her. 'Don't be long, little princess. I've got something special planned afterwards.' As he expected, it brought a smile to her lips and hugging the bear tightly, she went into the hospital building.

13

The Broken Heart

'You say your name is Lindidwe Loma?

'Yes.'

'How old are you?'

'Eighteen years . . . nearly nineteen.'

'Where do you live?'

'With Richard Zondi at . . .'

'We want your home address, not Zondi's.'

'I . . . I can't tell you that.'

Police Captain Enok Meewa sighed and put down his pen. 'Lindidwe,' he said gently, 'do you understand how serious your crime is?'

Lindi jumped up from her chair. 'No! I have done nothing wrong! Nothing. I want to see Richard. He will tell you that . . . he'll tell you this is all a terrible mistake! Where is he? I want to see him!' She shivered and started to cry – great dry sobs that tore from her stomach and broke out in fits of hard coughing.

'Lindidwe . . . listen to me.' Enok came round and lifted her from her knees. 'There is no mistake. This man Zondi says he has never seen you in his life before. He says he doesn't know any girl called Lindidwe Loma.'

Lindi stared at him through her tears. 'You're lying! He loves me!'

'We have questioned him over and over. He says he does not know you . . . that you are the one who is lying.'

'I don't believe you! Let him tell me to my face that he doesn't know me!'

'Is that what you want?'

'Yes! Yes!'

Enok sighed and walked to the door. He said something to a policewoman who came in and took Lindi's arm.

'Go with her. When we have Zondi, we'll call you.'

Lindi pulled her arm away. 'Am I going to prison?' The shock and horror of what was happening was more than she could bear. This was all a terrible nightmare. Soon she would wake up and find the comfort of Richard's arms around her.

'You have broken the law,' Enok said. 'Take her away.'

Lindi fell to the floor, screaming. Another policewoman came and the two women pulled her to her feet.

'Tell Richard I want to see him!' she shouted as they dragged her away. 'You'll see! He'll get me out of this!'

Enok took off his glasses and rubbed his eyes. He was a short, thickset man with a kind heart and gentle manner. Right now he was tired and wanted more than anything to go home to sleep. He was sorry for Lindi and believed she was telling the truth and did not know anything. She had been used as a go-between for the gangster Richard Zondi but they could not prove it. The girl had been caught carrying dangerous drugs hidden in a toy bear. She was the guilty one and would have to pay for her crime.

He put his glasses back on and sighed. Then he picked up the telephone. 'Get Zondi here as soon as you can . . . if you can't find him? Wait . . . don't show yourself . . . he may take fright and try to get away . . . yes . . . yes . . . let me know as soon as you bring him in.'

———— ❤ ————

Late the next day, Lindi was brought back to Captain Enok Meewa's office. He frowned when he saw her. Her suffering had spoiled her beauty. Her eyes were swollen and puffy and there were scratches on her dirty face. Her hands and bare feet were also dirty and her hair stuck out in untidy knots about her head. He saw her dress was torn and also dirty.

'What happened? Who did this to you?' he asked quickly. Lindi hung her head and said nothing. Enok looked at the policewoman. 'It was the other girls in the cell, wasn't it?'

'Yes,' said the policewoman. 'They took her shoes and tried to take her dress but she put up a fight.'

'I'm sorry,' Enok said and pulled out a chair. 'Sit down, Lindi.'

Moments later Richard Zondi came through the door. 'You have no right to force me in here!' he shouted. 'I have made a statement and there's nothing more to be said.'

'Richard!' Lindi jumped up and ran to him, throwing her arms around his neck. 'You came at last! I waited . . . I begged them to let me see you!' She was laughing and crying at the same time, pressing kisses to his face. But Richard stepped back and pushed her away.

'Get your dirty hands off me!' He slapped her away from him and cursed. 'Who do you think you are? I've never seen you before!' He pushed her so hard, she fell.

'Richard!' Lindi screamed. 'What are you saying? How can you act like this? It's me . . . Lindi . . . Look at me!' She was on her knees, her arms around his legs, sobbing loudly. 'Richard . . . tell them this is all a terrible mistake! I have done nothing bad . . . tell them! Tell them! Please tell them so we can go home . . .'

Richard kicked her away, his boot cutting open her cheek. She put her hand to her face and looked in horror at the blood staining her fingers.

'Are you mad?' She stared at him in shock and disbelief. 'How can you do this to me! And why? Why, Richard? Why?'

'I don't know what you're talking about. I don't know you and I don't know what your game is. The police got you for carrying dope and now you're trying to put the blame on me! Look at her!' He turned to Enok and pointed at Lindi. 'Do you think I would ever go around with a cheap, filthy whore like her? You think I'd be that crazy?'

73

Enok looked at Richard's expensive clothes and the gold jewels that flashed on his wrists and fingers. 'I don't know what is the truth and what is a lie. That is for the judge to decide. Now get out, Zondi.'

'No! Richard, don't leave me! Don't let them throw me in gaol! I've done nothing wrong! Richard . . . I beg you! Don't go like this! I love you!' Richard took no notice. Without once looking back, he walked out the door and slammed it behind him.

———— ♥ ————

The magistrate looked at Lindi over the tops of his black framed glasses. He was a big man with a kind heart and felt pity for the trembling young girl staring at the floor in front of him. Lindi was dressed in a blue prison overall. She had white canvas shoes on her feet and her head was covered with a blue scarf. She had lost a lot of weight and looked weak and sick. Captain Meewa was with him and gave him Lindi's case file. The magistrate looked at the file and said, 'I have a full police report on your case Lindidwe, but I want you to tell me in your own words . . . one . . .' he held up a finger, '. . . why you were carrying drugs and . . . two,' he held up the next finger, '. . . how you were caught and arrested. No, let's make a number three . . . why do you say you know this man Richard Zondi when he says he doesn't know you?'

'He lies.' Lindi's voice was dull and flat.

'Tell me what happened. If I hear it from you, it can help you a lot.'

Lindi did not look at the magistrate but kept her eyes on the floor and in the same flat voice told him everything. How she had been taken into Richard's house and how she had come to love and trust him.

'So not once did you think he was a crook? Or that Beauty and Alyce were not his sisters?'

'No.'

'What happened when you were arrested?'

Slowly and painfully, Lindi began to talk. She told the magistrate about the Fun Fair where Richard had got her the bear. How he had asked her to take the bear to Alyce who was sick in hospital. At this point the magistrate stopped her. He took out a sheet of paper and looked at it. Then he looked at her. 'Captain Meewa told you that there was nobody by the name of Alyce Zondi at the hospital. That it was all a lie, didn't he?'

Lindi nodded. 'I know all that.'

'What you don't know is that Alyce was found two days later.' He looked at Lindi and waited. When she said nothing he went on. 'She was found dead on a railway line. At first it was thought that a train had hit her. Later it was found she had died from a gunshot wound in her head.'

'Alyce . . . dead?' Lindi was shocked.

'She was dead before the train hit her. This means that somebody threw her across the railway line to make it look like an accident or maybe even suicide.'

'Do the police know who killed her?' Lindi asked in a whisper.

The magistrate shook his head. 'No. Maybe they never will. Organised gang murders are not easily solved. It can take months . . . sometimes years.' He put the paper away and asked, 'What happened when you got to the hospital?'

'I left Richard in the car and walked to the big hospital doors . . .'

'With the bear?'

'Yes, but then somebody knocked me down from behind and ran off with the bear. Richard saw it happen and ran after him. He came back later with the bear and said he had caught the man who stole it. He still wanted me to go and see Alyce and gave me back the bear but . . . the bear didn't feel the same. I thought it looked different but I wasn't sure.'

'In what way did it look different?'

'The bear Richard gave me at the Fair was very furry and new but the bear he got back from the man who stole it was smoother because I remember stroking its fur and thinking the fur was not so fluffy but more thin and short.'

'So why did you not say this in your statement? Why tell me now?'

'Because I thought I just made a mistake because why would Richard give me a different bear?'

'Did you think about it after that?'

'No . . . I was worried I would get lost in that big hospital so I went through the doors and when I was going to speak to a nurse, this man came and stopped me. He said he was a policeman and he wanted me to go with him. I went with him into a small office and he took the bear away. He said . . . he said they had a . . . tip-off . . . I think he called it that . . . and the bear I was carrying had drugs hidden in it. He said he had to make sure this was true.'

'And then?'

'He told me to wait until he got back.'

'And you believed him?'

'Yes, because he was wearing a policeman's uniform and he showed me a government book full of stamps and things . . .'

'How long did you wait?'

'Not long. The next thing Captain Meewa came into the room and he was carrying the bear. He also told me that an informer had let them know about the drugs in the bear and where and when the exchange would happen.'

'That must have been when the thief knocked you down. He ran off with your bear and the bear Zondi brought back was a different bear – a bear stuffed with drugs. The whole thing had probably been planned long ago and they wanted to use you as an innocent go-between.'

'I swear I knew nothing about drugs or that . . . Richard

was a crook . . . I swear it!' She started to cry softly, her hands to her face.

'I believe you Lindidwe, but there is one more thing. Why will you not tell us the truth about where you live?'

'Because . . . because . . .' Lindi could not speak. Enok Meewa went to her and put his hand on her shoulder. 'Is it because you are ashamed?'

Lindi nodded. 'Mama and Baba will die if they know all this.'

'And this is the only reason?'

'Yes . . . I feel so ashamed and so sorry for everything that has happened.'

The magistrate looked at Enok. 'What do you think?'

'I believe she is innocent. She has suffered much these past weeks in prison . . . and we did get the drugs.'

'But not the man who said he was a policeman.' The magistrate shook his head. 'It can happen over and again. We never get the gangster . . . the big chief of the drug ring.'

Lindi stared at them. 'You didn't catch him? He's still free?' Her eyes grew wide with fear.

'If he finds me, he'll kill me.'

'No he won't. He was shot while trying to escape. He'll be too badly wounded to come and look for you.'

'But even so, what about the others? When I'm free they'll come after me!'

The magistrate shook his head again. 'No, don't worry. That's why they choose innocent girls like you. It's your word against theirs and if we can't prove anything, they get off free. It's victims like you that are caught by the police but also only if a police informer gives them a tip-off.'

'What will happen to me now?'

'You will be allowed to go free until your case comes up in court. But only if you can pay the bail money.'

'Bail? What is that?'

'A sum of money that is paid for you so you do not have to stay in prison.'

'How much money is that?' Lindi looked at the magistate through her tears.

The magistrate looked at a paper in her file and told her. Lindi felt as if somebody had hit her.

'It's a lot of money,' Enok Meewa said, 'but it's because your crime is so great. You are only proved innocent at your trial.'

'I haven't got so much money,' Lindi cried.

'What about your family?'

'Never! I would rather die than ask them.'

'Somebody else then?'

'There is only . . .' But she could not say Sipho's name. 'No, there is nobody else.'

'Think about it. Maybe a name will come to you. Until then I'm sorry, but you will have to stay in your cell.'

It was over. Lindi found Enok Meewa looking at her in a way Richard had once looked at her. She knew he was sorry for her and that he believed her story but she did not need that kind of pity from anybody, no matter how alone and helpless she was. As the guard took her back to her prison cell, she thought of Sipho. How she had messed up her life! All along, Sipho had been right. She should have listened to him. Then she would have been with him now and none of these terrible things would have happened to her. She was nothing but a criminal. She was in prison and her fingerprints were on record for all time. Sipho had never written to her. Had he found somebody else to love? Maybe married? Her heart ached. She knew now how deep her love for him was and had always been. She had been tricked by a terrible evil spirit that had stolen her true love for Sipho and filled her heart with lies and darkness.

When the barred iron door slammed behind her, she threw herself down on the thin hard mattress and cried as if her heart would break.

14

Love Lies Lost

Sipho's mother shook her head sadly when she saw her son still bent over the account books. 'You work too hard, my son,' she said. It was nearly midnight and Sipho had been working since early dawn, ploughing and planting his fields.

'There is always a lot of work, Mother. The day is never long enough.'

'Then let Tombi help you. She will do anything for you. You should not be the one helping me in the shop just because your sister has gone away with her new husband.'

'Tombi?' Sipho put down his pen and rubbed his tired eyes.

'Why not? She is always asking and she has a sharp head with figures.'

'That's true.' Sipho bent over the books. 'Let me think about it, but first I must finish this before I go to sleep.'

His mother sighed and went to her room. She blamed Nomsa's girl Lindidwe for the change in her son. Ever since the girl left, Sipho was like a lovesick bull. She had never been very happy about Lindidwe Loma. She was too beautiful with those strange slanted eyes and high cheekbones. Then she went and did something to her hair to make her different from the other village girls. She was also too thin. She should have had a baby by now – a fat, healthy boy. That would have put flesh on her bones and dulled the restless spirit in her.

Lindidwe. Even as a child, she was the one the other children followed. She always had new games to play, new hiding places to find and new playing grounds to explore. Now she was a grown woman and still running off to places unknown. Like Sipho's goats who broke fences or jumped over stone kraal walls – always hoping that on the other side they would find greener, sweeter grass to eat. Why had the girl not written to Sipho? Not even a few words of love to comfort his aching heart. There had only been the letter from the aunt and Nomsa and Petrus kept their lips sealed about that letter. It was all very strange. Maybe Lindidwe had found another man and they would not say. Sipho's mother was angry at Lindidwe for the suffering she was causing her son. Every day she saw the light in Sipho's eyes shine and then go out when no letter came. Now he expected nothing more. Instead, he worked like a man with the spirit of the devil in him. Work. Work. Work. It gave him no time to think and when he fell on his mattress at night, he would quickly fall asleep. Only his mother did not know that even in his sleep, Lindidwe came to trouble his dreams.

———— ♥ ————

Tombi leaned against a tree and looked at Sipho from the corner of her eye. 'She has forgotten you,' she said with a sly, secret smile. 'There is a new man in her life and that is why she hasn't written to you.' Sipho cursed. It was true. Everybody in the village knew that he had received no letter. It was the way with village people. There were those who felt sorry for him and spoke in whispers behind their hands. Sipho Sosibo was a fool. Big, strong, young and handsome, he had enough money to raise a fine, healthy family. There were many other girls he could choose to marry. Girls who would make a better wife and mother than Lindidwe. Who could say what she would be like when she came back from the city? She might want a big house, fancy furniture and all the good things money could buy. She would soon make Sipho a poor man if she did not work him to death first. So the village talk went on, day after day because there was no letter for Sipho and Nomsa and Petrus stayed tight lipped. All the village people knew was that only one letter had come from Nomsa's sister in Bethsada but Nomsa had taken it to Old Granny to read. Nobody would dare to question a *sangoma* about the secrets of those who went to see her.

'Sipho . . . you sleep alone and your arms are empty. Is there a place for me in your heart?' Tombi gave him a shameless wink and pressed against him. 'It's been a long time since Lindi left and . . .' she looked him up and down . . . 'you are a man whose blood runs hot.'

'You are shameless! If you want me you will wait until cows grow wool and sheep breed calves!' Sipho pushed her aside and walked off. Tombi laughed. There had to be a way to his heart. Maybe Old Granny could help.

———— ♥ ————

Sipho went to visit Old Granny many times after Lindi went away. He took her gifts of maize meal, flour, sugar, soap and candles. Sometimes he also took her a kid goat, and a calabash of sour beer. They would sit around the smoking fire in the cave and talk about things past and things to come. She did not wear her animal skins and monkey tails then but a long black dress and a black silk shawl with a fringe.

Today she was dressed as a *sangoma* and when Sipho limped into her cave at sundown, she was waiting for him.

'Are you expecting somebody?' Sipho asked and gave her a twist of chewing tobacco that she likèd.

'I am not expecting anybody, but these three nights past, I have been visited by a spirit of darkness that calls from far.' She shivered and pulled the ragged skin blanket more tightly over her shoulders. Sipho waited. 'It calls to you, *insiswe* and until I throw the bones for you and find this dark spirit, I will have no peace.'

Sipho stared at her. 'Is it . . . Lindidwe?'

Old Granny nodded. 'I fear it may be so.'

'Then throw the bones! If something is wrong . . . if she is in trouble, I must know!'

The *sangoma* closed her eyes. She pulled the bag out of the skin pocket between her breasts and tipped the bones out, rubbing them slowly between her claw-like hands. Chanting and moaning softly, she rocked backwards and forwards on her bare heels before she gave a loud cry and threw the bones to the ground.

Sipho looked at them. They were not all bones. There were also a few smooth, shiny stones, some sea shells, a baby tortoise shell and two very old coins. Old Granny poked around the bones with a stick and silent tears slid down her dry, wrinkled cheeks.

'What is it?' Sipho asked sharply. 'What do you see that makes you cry?'

Old Granny shook her head and slowly picked up the scattered objects and put them back into the bag. She was still crying – small animal sounds of pain and suffering.

'Tell me! What is wrong? What did you see?' Sipho begged, but the *sangoma* turned away. Without a word she left him kneeling in the dust and disappeared into the dark cave. Sipho knew she would not return that day. There was nothing he could do except go back home and wait till morning.

Old Granny had to tell him what she had seen in the pattern of the bones. Good or bad, anything was better than nothing. Lindi's silence was slowly and surely driving him mad.

———— ♥ ————

In a small, dirty prison cell, Lindi lay with her face to the wall. She had eaten nothing and felt weak and sick. She listened to the cockroaches running around the cement floor and shivered. The other girls in the cell were asleep. Nobody worried her any more. She had told them her grandmother was a *sangoma* and that she too, had the gift. Fear of her curses made them leave her alone.

In the quiet, lonely hours of the night, Lindi cried for Sipho. She would at last fall asleep with his name on her lips and her love for him in her heart. What a fool she had been! Now she was being punished for betraying his love and trust. She knew now that he had never received her letters. Richard had found her second letter lying on the hall table and said he had posted it for her. It had been a lie. Beauty had also lied when she said she had posted her first letter. Had they lied about her aunt as well? She did not know. She only knew she had caused the only man she truly loved much pain. How he must have suffered when he never got any letters. What would his thoughts have been? Auntie must have written to her parents. What would they be thinking of her?

She had caused everybody to suffer because of her selfish greed. Would they ever forgive her and give her another chance? Her thoughts went over and over in her head until she wanted to die rather than live and face her shame. How could she write to them from a city gaol? It was much worse than being dead. So it was that her silent cries of grief and regret flew through her prison bars and like the ghostly drumbeats of Sipho's love, were carried by the wind to the troubled night world of Old Granny's dreams.

15

Free to Love?

In nights of deep velvet, the heart of Africa throbbed with life. By morning, dusty fields spread a lacework of spider's webs over the dew-wet earth. Tiny beads of water glittered like diamonds on the lace – a gift of beauty to the rising sun.

Sipho's boots carved dark patterns on the damp dusty footpath to Old Granny's cave. A man of the land, sun and sky, today his eyes were blind to nature's rich tapestry of life as he limped along the path. They were blind also to the imprints of small bare feet that had beaten him to the cave. Sipho's deepest thoughts were only on the truth that would wipe out the lies about his heart's love now trapped between darkness and evil. He did not see eyes bright with fun and trickery watch him limp to the mouth of the cave. Eyes that saw the mask of hurt and worry on his face and then disappeared behind a rock until he passed by. 'Your pain is like a wound full of pus . . . it needs to be cut and soothed and I will be the one to make everything better . . .' Silent as a cat, Tombi followed Sipho into Old Granny's cave.

❤

Lindi was too weak to help the other women prisoners hoe the kitchen gardens. She was sent to the laundry to help sort out dirty towels and bed linen for washing and ironing. Even there she had to rest time and again. She was sitting on a narrow wooden bench, leaning against the wall, her eyes closed when somebody spoke her name. She opened her eyes and quickly got up. 'The nurse said I can rest . . .'

'Sit, Lindidwe . . . I want to talk to you.'

Captain Enok Meewa pushed her gently back on the bench.

'Has something happened? Am I in more trouble . . .?'

'Quiet . . . don't upset yourself . . . nothing's wrong.'
Enok spoke softly. He had never seen anybody as nervous
and frightened as Lindidwe.

'Then why have you come?'

'Lindidwe . . . Lindi . . . I want to take you out of here. It
is not the right place for a girl like you.'

'How can you? The magistrate said . . .'

'I know what he said. You need bail money to be free.'

'Until my . . . trial?'

'Yes.' Enok nodded then took her hand. He was so gentle
that she did not pull it away. 'I have a plan but it will cost
you something that has nothing to do with money.'

'A plan to get me freed?' She looked up at him with a light
of hope in her wide dark eyes.

'You want to be free don't you?'

'More than anything but . . . I will never get the money.'

'If you agree to my plan, you won't need any money.' He
squeezed her hand and let it go. 'I will pay your bail.'

'You?' Lindi looked at him in surprise. 'Why?'

'Because I believe you are innocent and because I feel sorry
for you and because . . .' Enok looked into her eyes. 'Because
I can't stop thinking about you. I want you to come and live
with me when you get out.'

Lindi drew a quick breath and stood up, swaying a little. 'I
should have known there would some trick in this.'

'It's no trick, Lindi.'

'And your wife? What will she say?'

'I am not married.'

'Why me?' Lindi knew she should have been excited but
suddenly she felt very tired and cheated. 'I thought you were
being a friend to me,' she whispered. 'But you want me to go
and live with you . . . sleep with you . . .'

'Is that so terrible? I am a kind man and I will be gentle
and patient with you. You are not like city girls. There is

85

something different about you and also . . . you are very beautiful.'

Lindi gave a short laugh. 'I am not beautiful. I am thin and sick and my skin is dull and scabby. Soon my hair will crawl with lice!'

'That is why you must leave this place. You are too good to be thrown in with the others. They belong here for their crimes . . . you don't.'

'It's true . . . I am innocent.'

'Then say you'll do it. Come live with me. I will be good to you, I swear. With the right food, fresh air and the love I will give you . . .' He did not go on, but took both her hands in his, looking deeply into her eyes.

'And if I can't find a job? How will I pay you back?'

'I will not expect the money back. Stay with me and I will ask only your love in return.'

Lindi was silent. She thought of the prison cell with its dirt, cockroaches and the cruel and evil things that went on between the other women prisoners. She hated it – all of it. She longed to walk in space and sunshine and clean open air. She wanted to sleep in a clean, decent bed and wear pretty, clean clothes that fitted. Freedom. Was any price too great to pay for freedom?

'I'll do it,' she said softly and lowered her eyes so that her long lashes swept a dark shadow over her high cheekbones.

Enok pulled her to him then quickly let her go. 'You won't be sorry, Lindi. You need a man to care for you and I can make you very happy. You do like me, don't you?'

Lindi gave him a small smile. 'Yes, you are very kind.'

'I will be much more than that. You'll see . . . life will be very different for you from now and yes, you will make me a very happy man too.'

Without a further word, he turned and quickly walked away. Lindi did not feel happy or unhappy. She was going to be free of prison walls. That was the only important thing.

She felt nothing for Enok Meewa. Her love belonged to Sipho. One day she would go home and tell him how sorry she was for all the suffering she had caused him. That her love for him had never died. A love nothing and nobody would ever steal again.

———— ♥ ————

Sipho stood in front of Old Granny. 'It's true then. She loves another man.'

The *sangoma* sat on her heels in front of the smoking fire throwing small chips of wood into the flames. 'Why do you want me to twist the knife deeper into your heart? What good will come of it?' She was not happy that Sipho had come. He should respect her wish for silence.

'I only ask for the truth.'

'Then you have spoken it.' There was more, but she would not say it. The young man had suffered enough.

'My Lindi is sleeping with another man? Is that why you were crying when you read the bones, Old Granny? Because Lindidwe was betraying me with another man?'

Sipho felt his heart would burst. His Lindi! *Sthandwa*! Was it possible that this one time the bones were wrong?

'I know your thoughts, *insiswe* . . . but your head tells a lie that your heart knows is truth.'

'But she loved me! She has always loved me and I love her! More than my life!'

'Then you must change your life . . .'

'How can I? She lives in my dreams . . . in my heart! She is in the sunshine, the rain, every tree, every blade of grass! I hear her laughter in the river . . . her voice in the songs of the wild birds . . . the softness of her body in the wind that caresses my flesh. How can I live without her?' Sipho covered his face and sank to the floor. Old Granny looked at him. 'Cry, Sipho . . . cry. It will wash away the pain and heal your heart. Cry . . . cry.'

She was not the only one to hear Sipho's great, tearing sobs. Tombi heard them too. She had come to beg for the *sangoma's* help in capturing Sipho's heart. Now that it was empty, she would do everything she could to fill the space. Before anybody could see her, she slipped out of the cave and ran all the way home.

16

Another's Love

Enok opened the door of his apartment and let Lindi in.

'Do you like it?' he asked, hoping she would be pleased with what she saw.

'It's very nice.' She looked around.

'If you want to change things, you can.'

'I like it just like this,' said Lindi.

'Then I want you to be happy here because it is your home now too.'

Lindi tried to smile. Everything was dead inside her and nothing was important. She had exchanged one prison cell for another but living with Enok was better than staying in gaol.

'Come, let me show you our bedroom.' He took her hand and led her into a room with a double bed, built-in cupboards, a dressing table and an easy chair. The room was not big enough for anything more. There were flowered curtains across the window that looked out over the street and the chair was covered with the same flowered material. So was the bed – a bed she would later share with him.

'First, I am going to cook you some fish, fried eggs and chips and give you lots of milk and cheese.'

'Not milk!' The way she said it made Enok look at her in surprise. 'Milk makes me sick . . . really sick . . .' Suddenly it was all coming back to her.

Richard . . . the glasses of milk and honey mixed with drugs . . . the look on his face when she told him she had poured the drinks into the toilet . . . the way she had thrown herself at him. She started to cry and ran from the room. Enok followed her.

'Softly . . . softly . . . there is no need to cry. I will not make you drink . . . or eat . . . anything you don't like.' He wanted to take her into his arms but did not. Instead, he patted her back and made her sit down on the couch in the lounge. 'What about tea? Do you like tea?'

She nodded through her tears.

'Then I will make us tea and yours without milk.'

She watched him get busy in the kitchen. He was not a young man nor was he handsome. His eyes were small and dark behind his wire framed glasses and his hands were also small for a man. He did not look like a police captain or a man hungry for a woman. He reminded Lindi more of somebody's kid uncle or Father Christmas without the white beard and red suit.

She was very tired. If only she could sleep and sleep and sleep. If only she could wake up and find herself in Sipho's house, sharing his bed, bearing his children. She drank her tea and watched him prepare supper. He was a good cook and when she first smelled the spicy fish cooking, the cramp in her stomach told her she had not been this hungry in a long time.

———— ♥ ————

A week passed. Lindi could not believe that Enok had not yet touched her. They slept in the same bed – he on his side and she on hers – like brother and sister.

He was kind and did everything to please her. When he was at work she stayed in the apartment, cleaning it and watching television. After the lunch hour she slept and watched more television. It kept her from thinking . . . thinking and thinking. So did sleep. She felt she could never get enough sleep. Enok spoke to her about his work and his hobby of collecting empty matchboxes. He showed her the model cars, aeroplanes and ships he had made from them. He always spoke to her in the same gentle voice and never asked her questions about her past. Nor did he ever offer to take her out anywhere. Lindi did not mind. She still had no life in her spirit and listened more than she talked. It was better that way.

Two weeks later he came home with a bunch of flowers and a bottle of wine. 'It's my birthday,' he said with a boyish laugh. 'Tonight I cook something extra special and we make it a special night.'

'You should have told me,' Lindi said shyly. She had nothing to give him except – without thinking, she kissed him on his cheek. 'Happy birthday, Enok.'

He looked pleased and went to open the wine. 'I am forty years old today . . . an old man.'

'That is not old,' Lindi said and put the flowers in a jar of water.

'Then let's drink to that,' he said and gave her a glass of the cold sparkling wine.

For the first time in many weeks Lindi felt a spark of life in her. The wine flowed through her body and took away the tightness and pain. She laughed and spoke more than she usually did. Her eyes were bright and her skin shone like new honey in the lamplight. Enok felt his blood rise and give way to desire. She looked so beautiful. He wanted her. He had waited long enough.

After the birthday dinner, they watched a funny movie on television and laughed together. When it had ended, she said she was tired and would go to bed. 'Are you coming?' It was the first time she had ever asked him and Enok was pleased. He had not tried to touch her once during this special time together. She trusted him and he believed his patience would be well rewarded.

'You go,' he said.

She stood in the doorway and looked at him, the light from the bedroom shining through her thin, cotton dress. She had put on weight and her body was curved and full. Enok's desire rose. He tried to look away. When she spoke, her voice was low and soft. 'Thank you, Enok. It was a very nice birthday dinner.' He nodded and took off his glasses, rubbing his eyes. 'You go on to bed,' he said gruffly. 'I'll come later.'

Lindi was nearly asleep when Enok came to her. She did not pull away or try to stop him. He had waited long enough and the time had come for her to pay the price for her freedom. Later she lay in the dark, tears slipping quietly down her cheeks. It was nearly dawn before she drifted into a deep and troubled sleep and when she woke up, Enok had gone.

———————— ♥ ————————

Enok went to work with a heavy heart. The night had started so well and ended so badly. If Lindi had fought him or hit him . . . anything . . . but Lindi had done and said nothing at all.

Like a yellow dog, he had slunk out of the apartment while she was still asleep. He did not want to see the look in her eyes when she woke up and saw him. He had wanted her so much and waited so long. Over and over he told himself that he had been patient . . . gentle . . . she could not feel any bitterness against him.

In his office, he took out her file. He read it again. She had suffered much at the hands of that devil Richard Zondi. Would her pain ever heal?

He knew nothing about Sipho because Lindi had never spoken of him. Was there somebody from her past? A beautiful girl like her? She would have had a man in her life. If only she would talk to him about her family and her life in the country. Enok sighed and closed the file. She had made a deal with him but he knew that it would be a very long time – if ever – before Lindi's spirit joined with his in the act of love.

17

Truth will out

When Sipho left Old Granny's cave, he knew he had to see the secret letter Nomsa had received from her sister in Bethsada. Until now, Nomsa and Petrus had said nothing. They went about their day to day business with the secret locked in their hearts. Sipho had respect for their secrecy but now he was burdened with the bad news the *sangoma* had told him in her round-about way.

He found Nomsa sitting in the sun next to her husband. She had a basket of peas on her lap and Petrus was helping her to shell them. Nomsa was not happy to see him. Ever since the letter had come, she had tried to stay out of his way. When she saw his face – the hard line of his jaw and the way his lips pressed together – she knew that today he had come for the truth.

His greeting was short and he did not smile. 'There has been no word from Lindidwe these many weeks,' he began. 'Not to me or to you.' He waited but they said nothing. Nor did they look at him as they went on quietly shelling the peas. 'I know something is wrong and it is time I know what it is. There have been no letters . . . only the one you have kept hidden.' Still they said nothing. Their silence hardened his heart. He would not leave until he knew the truth.

'I have spoken to Old Granny . . .'

Nomsa looked up quickly. 'She will say nothing!'

'About the letter? No, but because her spirit has been troubled by Lindi's silence, she cast the bones for me.'

'Why you? We are her parents . . . why did Old Granny not send for us?' Nomsa was upset but Petrus said quietly, 'It is not for us to question the ways of a sangoma.'

'But we are Lindidwe's parents, old man! We have a right to know if there is trouble with our daughter . . .'

'And I have the same right if I am still the man she has promised to marry!' Sipho cut in. 'I have come to you for that reason. I want to see the letter that came from Bethsada.'

'It does not concern you, Sipho. It is a private letter from my sister.'

'It is also about Lindidwe.' Sipho looked at Petrus. 'You are a man like me . . . your thoughts would be the same as mine. It is time I learnt the truth.'

Nomsa got up and went inside the house, taking the basket of peas with her, but Petrus called her back. 'Sipho is right. Show him the letter.' He started to cough painfully.

Sipho waited. If Nomsa did not agree – but just as he got up to go after her, she came out with the letter in her hand. It was crumpled and dirty from the many times she had held it in her hands.

After today, Sipho would want nothing more to do with their daughter. Nomsa was deeply ashamed. Sipho was a good man. She had kept the secret for so long hoping that Lindidwe would write and make everything better. Now it was too late. They would lose a fine son-in-law and who could tell what kind of daughter the city would give back to them?

'Take it, but do not read it here. When you have done with it, leave it with your mother at the store. I will get it there.'

Sipho took the letter and without another word, left them. He limped along the river path to the rocks where the water ran like Lindi's laughter. He wanted to be near her when he read the letter.

———— ♥ ————

Lindi looked at the torn sheet of paper in her hand. She had started to write to Sipho but the words would not come. Unless she wrote a pack of lies, there was nothing she could say that would comfort their hearts.

Enok was late coming home and she knew why. Lindi was not angry with him. She had made an agreement and she would keep to it but he would never win a place in her heart. When at last she heard his key in the lock, she was there to meet him.

'You are not cross with me?' were his first words.

'No.' Lindi took his briefcase. 'I agreed to come and live with you, Enok. You did not force me to do anything against my will and also . . . you have been very patient with me.'

When he put his arms around her she did not pull back but he could feel the stiffness in her body. It did not worry him. In time she would come to love him and Enok was a patient man. He had as much time as it would take to win her love and father their child.

———— ♥ ————

It was nearly dark and Sipho was still at the river. He had read the letter not once, but many times. Slowly the pain and heaviness in his heart began to harden like the rocks in the riverbed. He heard the water rushing over them like the sound of Lindi's laughter . . . laughing at him . . . laughing and laughing.

Suddenly he grabbed one of the loose rocks lying at his feet and with a loud cry threw it as hard as he could at the rushing, rippling waters. He picked up another . . . and another . . . throwing them faster . . . faster . . . smashing them against the big wet rocks that stood as solid and strong as his love for Lindidwe had been. When he lost his footing and fell into the water, he smashed his fists against those same rocks until his hands were scratched and bleeding.

'Lindi! I have loved you so much! Lindi! My heart! My life! I have given you the heartbeat and breath of my body! Why have you done this to me? Why? Why? Lindeeeee!' With broken hearted curses he half crawled, half dragged himself back to the river bank, the water mixing with his tears. Never again would he shed tears for the love of a girl. Lindidwe Loma had gone from his heart and nobody would ever take her place or cause him pain again.

———— ♥ ————

Lindi woke suddenly. Sipho had called her name. There was no mistake about it. Sipho had come to her in a dream but his cry had been very real – so real it frightened her. Something had happened to him and in his desperate hour he had called her name. The cry had been loud and clear. Lindi! She looked at Enok snoring softly next to her. He had heard nothing.

Deeply troubled and unable to go back to sleep, she lay quietly in the dark. How much longer could she live not knowing whether Sipho was all right and that his love for her was as deep and binding as the last time they had been together? In his sleep, Enok shifted his weight closer and drew her against him. Lindi made a decision. Every time Enok came to her, she would close her eyes and pretend he was Sipho. It would make things easier between her and Enok and she could dream more and more of her lover in Kwamakutha.

If Lindi thought she could fool Enok, she was wrong. From the time she made up her mind to play her game of make-believe he got to know about the man who held her heart captive. She did not know that Sipho's name escaped her lips when she cried out in the dark. Enok knew finally that no matter how patient he was with her or how much time he gave her, she would never truly be his.

She became restless and ate little, picking at her food and hardly speaking. Her rounded curves were becoming sharper, her hip bone digging uncomfortably into him when they lay together.

'You must go out more,' he said to her one morning before he left for work. 'It isn't good that you stay here day after day.'

'I keep busy,' Lindi said quickly. 'There is always washing and ironing and . . .' She did not want him to know that she lay and slept much of the day. It was her way of escaping her thoughts. '. . . cleaning,' she ended softly.

Enok got up from the breakfast table and put his arm around her. 'Lindi . . . if it were possible, you know I would let you go home for a short time but while you are on bail you are not allowed to leave Bethsada.'

'I understand. It's just that . . . Enok? Will you do something for me?' She suddenly had an idea. 'Will you write a letter to my parents and let them know I am all right?'

Enok was surprised. 'Why me? Why don't you write to them?'

'Because I am too ashamed. I have not written to them since . . . a long time ago and I don't even know if they got the letter. Nobody wrote back to me. If they don't hear from me they might . . . they might think I'm dead or something.'

Enok did not laugh at her sad and serious face. The letter was important to her but whether it was going to be more important to her boyfriend he did not know. Maybe this was going to be another letter that would not be posted.

All that day Lindi thought about the letter she would get Enok to write for her. She walked back and forth, from the window to the door and back again. Her thoughts went round and round in her head until it ached. When Enok came home later that day, she had changed her mind. There was to be no letter after all.

18

This Man will be Mine!

Sipho did not know that Tombi followed him whenever she could. She did so without him knowing. She badly wanted a chance to be alone with him long enough to show him that she was more than willing to take Lindi's place. But she did not know that he was afraid to be alone.

On the day he took the letter from Nomsa she followed him to the river. Hidden in a thick clump of thorn trees, he did not see her but she saw his grief. She knew it had something to do with Lindi. Everybody in the village knew that Nomsa's letter from her sister had news about Lindidwe that they would not speak about. It meant that the news was bad.

Tombi, watching Sipho's anger and bitterness, did not feel sorry for him. She was glad. More and more, the time was coming closer for her to make her move. She had to see the letter, but how? Once she had read the letter she would know for sure whether or not Lindi was coming back to Kwamakutha. It would give her more time and she needed time if she was going to take Lindi's place in Sipho's heart. She knew he hated her but hate and love were two seeds in the same pod. Whether Sipho took her in lust or love, she would bear his child and love would be born in the son she would give him. Tombi would make sure of that. First, she had to get her hands on the letter.

In the end, it was easier than any trickery she had ever planned. The letter was lying on the shop counter where Sipho had left it for Nomsa to collect. Tombi could not believe her luck. She was about to pick it up when Sipho's mother saw her.

'Tombi,' she said and picked up the letter. 'Nomsa is

supposed to come and fetch this letter. If she comes in and I miss her, will you see that she gets it?'

Tombi, who helped out at the shop from time to time, nodded. 'I will put it where I won't forget,' she said and put the letter next to the money till. 'Are you going out?' Sipho's mother had taken off her apron and was carrying her plastic shopping bag.

'I have to take Sipho something to eat. He is out working in the fields today.' It would have been easier to ask Tombi to do it but she knew her son did not like Tombi. Tombi was only too glad to be alone. It would give her plenty of time to read Nomsa's letter. She watched Sipho's mother walk off towards the field where Sipho was working and without wasting a minute, she opened the letter and smoothed it flat.

———— ♥ ————

A sharp knock on his office door made Enok look up from the report he was writing out.

'Come in,' he called, putting down his pen. At the same time he took off his glasses and rubbed the lenses against his pants leg before putting them back on to see who it was.

The young police sergeant who came forward had a sheet of paper in his hand.

'I thought you would want to see this straight away, Captain Meewa,' he said and put the paper on Enok's desk. Enok read the paper and, without a word, gave it back to the disappointed young sergeant.

'Don't you want to follow this up, Captain?' he asked in surprise. 'We thought it important enough to . . .' Enok did not let him finish.

'It is important, Sergeant, but so is this report I am writing. Much more important than that pig dying from a knife wound in his stomach. Pigs like him can take a long time to die. I will attend to him personally in one hour.'

Enok needed the time. If the report was true and the dying

man confessed, it was very possible that Lindi would be free. Free to leave Bethsada . . . free to go home . . . The thought hurt him. He had come to love her quiet, gentle ways even though he knew she was unhappy – a willing prisoner in his home. But he knew he could not keep the news from her. Sooner or later she would know the truth, especially if there was to be no trial. He sat with his head in his hands, staring at the report in front of him, seeing nothing but her sad thin face. The girl was very homesick. She never complained nor did she ever say anything about her family or the man she had left behind. Now everything had changed and, like a man, he would have to be honest enough to take the chance of whatever would happen. He could not keep the truth from her – the truth that would at last set her free to go home to her family and . . . this hurt him more than anything . . . the lover who waited for her.

———— ♥ ————

Dear Sister . . . Tombi read. *This letter is very hard for me to write but it must be done. Your daughter Lindidwe is not here with me as it was planned. She was not at the railway station on the day I was there to meet her and later when I went to a lot of trouble to find out what had happened to her, the conductor said he had made a mistake and put her off at the wrong station. By the time I was able to get to this station, it was already dark and I could not find Lindidwe anywhere* . . . Tombi laughed, glad that Lindidwe had got lost.

She skipped over the next few lines that had been crossed out and read further . . . *I could not believe it when the next morning this strange man in a suit and tie drove up to my house in a car so smart and fancy, all the people in the street came to stare. They thought the president himself had come to see me.* Tombi sighed and skipped some more lines. So far the letter told her nothing she wanted to know. Then her eyes narrowed and she read slowly and carefully, *It seems that Lindidwe went home with this stranger when it got dark. She stayed the night with him and his two sisters and, Nomsa . . . he told me that Lindi was so happy there that she wanted to stay a few days before she came to me. He gave me a short letter she had written to say this was true. Her new friends are very rich and have promised to give her a good time. Would I mind if she stayed a while longer . . . Then he took back the letter before I could get over my shock and surprise and put it in his coat pocket. I did not dare ask for it back. He was a very handsome young man, Nomsa, and he said that he and his sisters would be very happy to have a beautiful girl like Lindidwe in their home and show her how different life in the city was. He looked me up and down as if I was dirt and said that Lindidwe would telephone me when she was ready to leave them. Now you know I do not have a telephone, Nomsa, and I did not like the man. Rich or not, he had no good manners and should have treated an old lady like me with respect even if I am not rich like him.* Tombi laughed. Smelly old she-cat . . . who would want to respect her – poor or rich? But if Lindi was having a good time . . . She read on. *It is now two weeks and I have heard nothing more. If Lindidwe is so happy with her new rich friends and too busy with her new life to think with respect about me, then I am sorry for you, my sister, but I will not welcome her in my house when she comes. It is better she goes home. When I see her . . . if I see her . . . I will tell her so.* There were more lines written and scratched out but Tombi did not bother to read anymore. She folded the letter and put it back next to the money till. So! Lindi was having the time of her life in the city with a rich, handsome young man who thought she was beautiful! She was no longer surprised at the way Sipho had taken the news. He deserved the pain Lindi had caused him. Fool! To waste his love on a cat like her! Girls like Lindi belonged in the city. For all Tombi cared, she could stay there and rot. Sipho was too good for her. Now more than ever, she would go about softly, softly worming herself into Sipho's heart. Before Lindi came back – if she came back – she would have Sipho in her bed and Lindidwe out of his life forever.

19

Innocence Proved

Enok looked down on the man in the hospital bed. Enok felt no pity for Richard Zondi. He deserved to die. This man had stripped an innocent country girl of all that was decent and left her to a fate worse than he was suffering now.

'How did this happen?' Enok asked the police officer next to him.

'He was stabbed in the stomach while playing poker, Captain.'

'For cheating?'

'Not this time, Captain. It seems that while Zondi was collecting his prize money, a girl came screaming at him with a knife. Something about Zondi having cheated her father and thrown them on to the streets without pity. Her father had killed himself because of it and she wanted revenge. Before anybody could stop her, she stuck the knife into Zondi's stomach.'

'What happened to the girl?'

'Shot in the head by one of Zondi's men.'

Enok sniffed, took off his glasses and rubbed his eyes. 'Now it's your turn, Zondi. Live by violence and you die by violence, isn't that right?' He put his glasses back on and saw Richard's eyes flicker and his mouth open.

'He wants to say something . . .' The police officer had his notebook ready when the doctor came into the ward. He took a quick look at the dying man and said, 'He hasn't much time . . . he's on his way out.'

Enok bent over Richard. 'Remember Lindidwe Loma?'

Richard's eyes flickered and closed. With all the strength he had left, he tried to speak. '. . . Lin . . .'.

'Yes, Lindi . . . she was arrested for carrying a toy bear stuffed with drugs and you knew all about it, you dog!'

Richard's eyes were closed. The doctor looked at the heart monitor next to the bed. 'He's fading . . . I'm sorry. I don't think he can hear you any more.' For a mad moment Enok was glad. If Richard did not clear Lindi's name, she would still stand trial. She would not leave him to return to the village where her lover waited.

'Look, sir! His lips are moving . . .' The police officer bent his ear to Richard's mouth. Frowning deeply, he tried to catch the broken words. '. . . Lin . . . di . . . inn . . . Lindi inno . . . cent . . .' A bloody froth burst from his mouth and he tried to cough. '. . . Lin . . . inn . . . o . . . cent . . . did . . . not . . . not know . . .' The beeper on the monitor suddenly went wild and sounded the death alarm. The wavy lines on the screen faded and slowly settled into a still, straight line. Richard Zondi was dead.

That same day Enok saw the magistrate.

'You know what this could mean, don't you?' The magistrate looked at Enok over the tops of his glasses. 'If Zondi's partner in crime can be found and made to confess Lindidwe's part in the drug deal, I believe she won't have to go to trial.'

'I have my men watching Zondi's house. There's a woman who lived with him. We'll keep a round-the-clock guard on the place until we find her.'

Enok was downcast that day when he went home. For Lindi's sake he knew he should be very happy. He decided not to say anything to her until he knew more. He did not want to raise false hopes and he was not looking forward to seeing the joy on her face when she was told she was free to go home.

If Lindi noticed that Enok was more quiet than usual that night, she said nothing. Later, when they went to bed it was the first time in many days that Enok did not touch her. She had done nothing wrong nor said anything to make him cross, but when she turned her face to the wall, she could not stop her tears and cried herself to sleep.

The next day Enok surprised her by coming home in the middle of the morning.

'Are you sick?' she asked quickly and went to fill the kettle for tea.

'No, I'm well . . . leave the tea, Lindidwe. I've come to take you to the police station.'

Lindi felt the blood rush to her face and put her hands to her cheeks, looking at him with wide, frightened eyes.

'Is it time for me to go to . . . court?'

Enok put a comforting arm around her. 'No, not that. This is something else, something that should make you very happy. But first I must tell you . . .' Enok watched her closely. 'Lindi . . . Richard Zondi is dead.' He was not sure how she would take the news of his death.

Lindi drew a quick, sharp breath and he saw shock take the place of fear in her eyes. Once again, she covered her face with her hands and bowed her head. It lasted only a moment and when she looked at him, her eyes were dry and her voice dull. 'When . . .? how . . .?' She took a deep breath. 'How did it happen?'

'He died from a stab wound . . . in hospital. I'm sorry, Lindi.' This time when he tried to comfort her, she pulled away. She felt limp and empty inside. There was no sorrow, no pity. He was dead. She would never see him again. She went and sat on the edge of the couch, her head bowed, her hands hanging between her knees. Enok went and sat next to her. 'That's not all, Lindi. Before he died he cleared your name. It wasn't much of a statement but it was a start. That's why I want you to come with me. There is somebody who wants to see you before she makes her own statement in this case.'

'A woman?'

Enok nodded. 'She says she will say nothing until she can speak to you.'

'Who is she?'

'Nobody to be frightened of. Don't worry, you won't be alone with her. I'll be there and so will one or two others.'

All the way to the police station, Lindi was silent and Enok respected her need to think things over. The prison held too many bad memories for her and the sooner she got out again, the better. She was nervous and frightened. As soon as they walked into a small, bare room at the end of the corridor and the door closed behind them, Lindi saw her.

'You!' Lindi wanted to run from the room but Enok held her arm. The girl and the woman stared at each other in a moment of silence and Beauty was the first to speak. 'Yes, Lindidwe it's me!'

'I never thought I would see you again . . .' Lindi felt sick. This was not the Beauty she remembered. This woman who looked at her with dull, grey eyes was thinner, shabbily dressed and dirty. She no longer had the long, braided and beaded hair; her head was bare, covered only with a thick black fuzz. She looked old and ill. 'You know about Richard? They told you?'

'We haven't got all day, woman . . .' Enok broke in impatiently. 'You know why Lindidwe is here. Now speak.'

As though she found breathing difficult, Beauty slowly told Lindi the real reason why she had been brought to Richard's house. The lie about her aunt and the letters that were never posted. Richard's love that was all a lie . . . the drugs in the drinks and his part in gang warfare and criminal dealings . . . the part she was to have in it – without ever knowing or agreeing to anything that might be against the law.

'Then Alyce was telling the truth!' Lindi cried. 'She tried to warn me . . .'

'That was why Richard killed her,' Beauty said.

'Richard killed her?' Lindi's eyes were wide with shock. She turned and pressed her head against Enok's chest. He put an arm around her.

'You did not know it was all a set up,' Beauty went on. 'You were never to know.' She got up slowly, as if in pain and went up to Lindi. 'You are innocent of any crime and I am the guilty one. I don't care any more. They can do to me what they like. Richard is dead and so are Alyce and Patrick, and others like me have been arrested.'

'Patrick is also dead?' Lindi asked, her voice rising. 'Then they'll kill me too! We'll all die! Those gangsters will never leave me alive if they know!' She clung to Enok. 'What am I going to do? I'll never get away free!'

Enok tried to calm her but it was Beauty who put her hand on Lindi's arm. 'No, you will be safe. Nobody but the Boss knew about you and he doesn't care now that Richard's dead. Nobody cares about a silly kid who will be only too happy to go back to digging sweet potatoes in some forgotten little village somewhere.'

Her words stung Enok. He knew that what she said was true. He had heard enough. 'Take her away,' he said shortly. Beauty went out with a policewoman on either side of her, a bent and ageing woman who did not care whether she lived or died.

Enok took Lindi back to the apartment and to her surprise, told her he was taking the rest of the day off.

'Lindi . . . we have to talk.' He took her hand and led her to the couch, sitting down next to her. Still holding her hand, he said quietly, 'You will soon be free to go home. Back to your family and . . . Sipho.'

Lindi pulled her hand away in surprise. 'I never told you about Sipho!'

'You didn't have to. Many times when we made love, it was his name on your lips, not mine.'

Lindi's face burned with sudden shame. 'I didn't know.'

'You must love him very much,' Enok said, his glasses suddenly misting over. He took them off and rubbed his eyes. Lindi did not want to hurt Enok. She took his hand and softly stroked the back of it, her eyes lowered.

'I have loved him since I was a small child. He is my life.'

'Then you will be married?'

Lindi nodded shyly. 'If he will still have me. I am hoping that his love will be great enough to understand.'

'He will understand and no man who has won the heart of a beautiful girl like you will not forgive you.'

Lindi did not reply. She was not as sure. Sipho was a proud man and no matter how much he loved her, he would never allow any woman to make a fool of him. She had a lot of explaining to do.

All at once she noticed Enok's shoulders shaking and his head in his hands. Enok Meewa was crying. She turned and put her arms around him so that his head rested in the hollow of her shoulder.

'I will never forget your kindness, Enok. I have loved you like a brother and one day I will give my son your name because of what you have done for me.'

In the growing darkness of the room, they sat holding each other; Lindi rocking him gently in her arms, like a small boy who needed to be comforted because of his pain.

20

Going Home

'So you are going home. You must be very happy.' The old woman in the train gave Lindi a toothless smile. She looked Lindi up and down, shaking her head. 'You're too thin, child. No man likes to hold a sack of bones to his heart. They like their women soft and plump like doves.'

Lindi looked out the window of the speeding train and said nothing but the old woman would not leave her alone.

'You got a man waiting?'

'No,' Lindi lied. 'I'm going home to my parents.' Lindi wished the old woman would be quiet.

'Hmmmm . . . they will say the same thing, you'll see. Too thin. Now when I was a young girl like you . . .'

Lindi let her talk. Every clack-clack-clackety-clack of the train wheels spinning along the railway track was taking her closer and closer to the man she loved. When Enok had put her on the train, she thought she would be the happiest girl on earth but once the train started moving homewards, fear took the place of joy.

She knew her mother and father would be happy to see her but would Sipho? She had told nobody she was coming home. If Sipho had another girl, it was better that she find out herself. All her hopes and dreams of a life with him depended on whether or not he still loved her and had waited for her. She looked at the lights that flickered past the window. Dark shapes and shadows that came and went as the train sped on to Kwamakutha. Would the old woman never stop her chattering? Lindi had so much to think about . . . . so much to plan about what she would say and do but the old woman went on and on and on! Suddenly Lindi could take no more.

'I'm tired . . . please . . . can't you see I want to be left alone?' She was close to tears as she got up and climbed on to the top bunk where she had left her things. She was grateful to Enok, not only for the train ticket, but also the bedding ticket. She crawled between the stiff white sheets and pulled the navy blue blanket around her shoulders. The train blew a long, lonely whistle into the dark, empty night and rattling along the track, slowly, gently, rocked her to sleep.

Very early the next morning the conductor tapped his metal key sharply against her door of the compartment.

'Hallo . . . hallo . . . hallo . . . your station's coming up in fifteen minutes, missy.' He slid the door open a little and poked his jolly face through the gap. 'Only stops a minute so be ready to jump off, OK?'

Lindi swung her legs over the side of the bunk and jumped down to get her belongings. The night sky was beginning to pale. She decided to leave the compartment and wait outside in the corridor. 'I'm coming home, Sipho . . . Mama . . . Baba, I'm coming home . . .' Tears filled her eyes. She had left Kwamakutha an innocent young girl. She was returning a woman. 'Sipho, if only you'd be there on the station waiting for me. How good it would feel to hold you and never, never let you go!' Her tears fell faster, blinding her to the country-side that flashed past – homeland she knew and loved so well.

When at last the train screeched to a stop, she got off. Nothing had changed. The station was the same. All that was missing were the people she loved. She stood on the platform long after the train had gone, a lonely figure next to her cheap cardboard suitcase, a canvas bag slung over her shoulder.

She rubbed her burning eyes and picked up the suitcase. The stationmaster was sure to be in his stuffy office, drinking coffee and listening to the early morning news on the radio. He lived along the same district road as her village and Lindi hoped he would be able to help her. Drawing a deep breath, she went to find him.

'You want a lift?' The stationmaster looked at the thin, sad faced girl who lowered her eyes and nodded. 'Well, you're lucky. My son will be bringing in the milk cans soon and when he goes back you can ride with him as far as the farm.' He looked at the clock on the wall. 'If you wait outside, you'll see him any time now.'

'Thank you very much, sir.' She shook her head when he offered her a mug of sweet, black coffee. The thought of food or drink made her sick.

Ten minutes later, a rusty dented farm truck pulled up outside the building. Lindi's lift had come.

———— ♥ ————

Petrus sat with his back to the early morning sun. He had just finished a bowl of yellow maize porridge with goat's milk and sugar. It was going to be another fine day. Not even the pain in his chest worried him this morning. The only thing wrong was he had no tobacco. Nomsa had said, 'No more tobacco, old man. It makes your cough worse. Suck the pipe if you must but that is all.' He sighed and stuck the empty pipe between his teeth.

Lindidwe would have given him a little tobacco on the side, he thought sadly. His daughter understood everything about him. Some day she would come home. He waved away the flies that worried him and kicked the dog at his feet. The dog yelped then pricked up its ears. Its long, whip-like tail began to swing.

'Now what's with you, dog? I kick you and you swing your tail at me, hey?' The dog whined softly, put its head to one side and then ran off with short, sharp barks. Petrus narrowed his eyes against the bright morning light then half rose to his feet, the blanket falling from his shoulders. Somebody was coming. A girl with a suitcase on her head.

The dog was jumping wildly up at her, barking and spinning its tail in excitement. Were his old eyes playing tricks? Could it be? The pipe fell from his mouth.

'Mama?' he croaked. 'Mama . . . come quickly . . . I think our child . . .' His heart began to beat faster. 'Yes! Yes! It is! Our Lindi . . . our Lindi has come home!'

As fast as his old legs could carry him, he hobbled into the dusty road, his arms open wide in welcome. 'Lindi! Lindi! Mama! Come see! Come see! Our daughter . . . our child is home!'

Lindi dropped the suitcase and ran to greet her father, tears of joy running down her face. She flung her arms around him and sobbed like the little girl he used to comfort on his knee. 'Yes, I'm home . . . I'm home, Baba . . . and I'm never going to go away again!'

———— ♥ ————

'I did write to you but I know now you never got my letters,' Lindi said quietly. 'It is a long story and I can't tell you anything now. I know you have forgiven me but what must Sipho think of me?'

'There was a letter . . .' Nomsa was thinking of Sipho and how badly he had taken the news he had read in her sister's letter. 'From Auntie. It was not a good letter, Lindi.' Nomsa looked at Petrus who sucked hard on his empty pipe and said nothing.

'What did she say?'

Nomsa got up from the table and went to get the letter. 'Here . . . read it yourself.'

Lindi took the letter and opened it. As she read, her eyes grew wider and her lower lip trembled. She threw the letter on the table and jumped up. Her heart was beating fast and she felt hot and cold all over. What must Sipho think of her? Never receiving any word from her . . . not knowing where to find her and perhaps thinking and fearing the

111

worst. She put her hands to her face, shaking with shame and fear.

'I don't know what to say!' she cried. 'The truth has been twisted into a terrible lie! I never wrote to Auntie, not once! These people did take me in when I had nowhere to go but they also lied and cheated! At first I thought they were my friends but later . . .' She spread her hands and gave them a sad and hopeless look. 'I must find Sipho! I must tell him it was all lies! I did write! Not only the one time but again and when he didn't write back, I thought . . .' She turned and ran to the door. 'I must find him! I must talk to him!'

'Lindi, wait! Sipho is not here!'

Lindi stopped and stared at her mother. 'Where is he?'

'He went to buy cattle and will be back in a week. Come child,' Nomsa said and went to Lindi. She put her arm around Lindi's shoulders and led her back to the table. 'Drink your tea, and look, you have not touched your food. You are much too thin. Eat now and rest. A week is not long and by that time you will look and feel better.' Nomsa fussed and talked, but Lindi did not listen.

She drank her tea and ate the sweet potato dumplings without tasting anything. Sipho. Sipho. His name went round and round in her head. What pain she must have caused him! Why did he have to be gone now when she needed him more than ever before? Maybe she could go to look for him? Nomsa suggested Tombi might know where he was. 'She works at the store now, Lindidwe. She and Sipho see a lot of each other and Tombi's brother is buying goats and sheep for Sipho. They are good friends.'

Tombi and Sipho? Lindi felt a burning pain spread inside her chest. Tombi had always wanted Sipho. But Sipho hated her! He had always said she had no shame. Did he still feel that way? Lindi looked at her mother in silence and then ran from the room. There was only one way to find out.

———— ♥ ————

'You!' Tombi could not believe her eyes. 'When did you get back? Sipho did not tell me you were coming.' Her small brown eyes narrowed. 'If he knew you were coming he would never have left. He doesn't know you're here, does he?'

Lindi did not answer. 'I want to know where he is.'

The two girls stared at each other. Tombi could not believe it was the same Lindi. Her friend had always been slim. Now she was as thin as a reed. Her high cheekbones stuck out like shelves under her wide, slanted eyes that looked too big for her face.

'You've changed,' she said and without being kind added, 'I didn't know it was the fashion to be so thin.' Tombi herself had put on weight. Her cheeks were as shiny and round as her breasts and buttocks. A young, healthy male like Sipho liked women soft and round. Not long now and he would no longer say 'no' to her. She looked at Lindi and frowned. Why did she have to come back and spoil everything? Tombi had to think fast. She picked up a feather duster.

'How should I know where Sipho is?' She flicked the duster over the shop counter.

'My mother said you'd know.' Lindi grabbed the feather duster from Tombi and shook her hard. 'You've got to tell me. It's very important. Where has he gone to buy cattle?'

Tombi's brain worked fast. If she did not do or say something to keep Lindi from finding Sipho, all would be lost. Nobody was going to spoil her plans for her and Sipho.

'He's gone to Mr Botha's farm on the other side of Kwa-makutha,' she lied. 'The Mr Botha at Bok-Bok-Two, but . . .' Tombi pretended to be upset, 'he said he would first go on to Baruti and end up at Bok-Bok-Two before coming home.'

'Then maybe I'll wait for him there,' Lindi said, her heart beating fast. If she had to wait forever, she would.

After she left the shop Tombi's thick lips spread in a wide, happy smile. With Lindi safely out the way, Tombi would

113

have just enough time to get to Sipho. She needed only one night with him. He had been without a girl long enough and a man's flesh was weak. Far from home and alone, she would cook his meat and warm his bed. By the time Lindi came to know the truth, it would be too late. Sipho would never be able to lie and later, when the child came, Lindi would be out of his life forever.

21

A Lover's Search

'Kanczane Msomi is taking sacks of meal and flour to some people near Mr Botha's farm tomorrow. If you ask him, he will give you a ride there,' said Petrus.

'Sipho will not get to Mr Botha's farm until maybe two, even three days from now. You are lucky to get a lift but you have to wait,' said her mother sharply.

Lindi was silent. She had only just come home. She owed it to her father and mother to spend some time with them. Later, when Nomsa went down to the river with her friends, Lindi gave her father a small packet of pipe tobacco.

'Don't tell mama . . . but I know how much you miss it.'

Petrus patted her shoulder. 'You're a good girl, Lindidwe. By the time your mama comes back, the pipe will be empty and I will feel like a new man.'

Slowly, the sky behind the hills of Kwamakutha changed to a splash of red-gold and lilac and Lindi and her father were glad to be alone at last in the silence of the setting sun.

Sipho was watching the same setting sun from a campfire on the other side of Kwamakutha's hills. He had found an old shepherd's hut with most of the grass roof gone and the walls falling down. It would give him enough shelter and he wanted to be alone on the wide valley floor to drink in the beauty and magic of the dark and lonely African night. The two small herd boys he had brought with him were already curled up in their blankets, fast asleep. Even the long horned cattle he had bought were lying down, quietly chewing the cud.

He took the dented white coffee pot off the smoking fire and poured out half a mug of strong black coffee. He had done well. The cattle were in good condition and tomorrow he would make his last stop at 'Outspan' before going home. Home? Home had never been the same since Lindidwe had left. As grey and uninteresting as the young girls who tried to take Lindidwe's place. They soon learned to leave him alone. Except Tombi. She was like a tick embedded in the fat of a sheep's tail. No matter how hard he tried to get rid of her, she only crawled deeper into his life.

He sipped the coffee and looked up at the stars. The same stars Lindi could see wherever she was. He could not get her out of his mind. Nor could he believe that he would never again hold her in his arms. He tried to harden his heart, picturing her in the arms of a rich city boy who could give her anything except a love as strong and binding as his.

'Lindi! Lindi!' He could feel her softness in the wind that was starting to blow across the valley and her passion in the flames that suddenly leaped higher. With a loud curse, he threw the rest of the coffee on to the fire, grabbed a pot of water and threw that over as well. The flames died in an angry hiss, spitting ash and smoke. He stamped the heel of his boot on the hot coals and went into the hut to unroll his blanket.

———— ♥ ————

The next day Tombi went to the shop with a note in her hand.

'I am very sorry, Auntie,' she said to Sipho's mother, 'but I will not be able to work for two days.' She held out the note. 'This is from my grandmother. My grandfather is sick and she needs help.'

'I am sorry too, Tombi. Are you sure you only need two days?'

'I think so. If I have to stay longer, I will send somebody to let you know.'

Tombi did not waste any more time. She had to get to Sipho before Lindi found out that she had lied. She knew that Sipho would be spending the next day or two at 'Outspan'.

She heard the taxi hoot for her and ran faster down the footpath, puffing and sweating.

———— ♥ ————

Kanczane's wooden donkey cart was waiting for Lindi very early the next day. Kanczane flicked his short whip over the donkeys' backs and the little cart set off down the road. Lindi looked over her shoulder at the heavy bags of maize meal, flour, grain and bundles of wood packed into the back of the cart. The load was heavy and neither the donkeys nor Kanczane were in much of a hurry. It was hard for Lindi not to grab the whip and send the beasts galloping as if all the devils in the spirit world were after them.

'When do you think we'll get there?' she asked the old driver. Without saying a word, he lifted his shoulders and dropped them. 'Before it gets dark? Will we get there before then?' The old man nodded and cleared his throat, spitting into the side of the road. Lindi sighed.

Two hours later, when the sun was at its hottest, she said: 'Shouldn't you give the donkeys a rest? Look . . . over there is a stream. I would like to wash my face and have a drink of water.' She was pleased the old man did not argue. He went as far as the stream and let the animals loose. It was good to rest in the shade.

She opened the paper bag of food her mother had given her, and gave Kanczane some bread Nomsa had filled with curried mince and onions. 'Is it still far?' she asked and watched him eat.

Kanczane took his time swallowing the food. When he spoke his voice was dry and rough like somebody who never spoke much. 'I think somebody is waiting for you because you ask so many times.'

'Yes! It is very important that I see Sipho before he starts back home and I know for sure he will be on Mr Botha's farm tonight.'

Kanczane shook his head.

'You are wrong to think that.'

'Why? What do you mean?' Lindi looked at him in surprise. 'I know Sipho will be there.'

The old donkey driver looked at her with watery eyes. 'Sipho Sosibo will sleep at "Outspan" tonight. I had to leave grain there for his cattle.'

'Who told you this? How do you know?'

'Sipho. He was to herd the cattle to "Outspan" and the food had to be waiting there.' Kanczane nodded as he spoke.

Lindi could not believe it. She felt the blood rush to her face and she swallowed hard, her hand to her mouth. Tombi had lied to her. Why? Why had Tombi lied? There was only one reason. She wanted to get to Sipho first. Lindi looked at Kanczane who stared back, his mouth full of food. 'We must go back, old man!' She got up quickly. 'There has been a mistake!' But hard as she tried, she could not get the donkey driver to turn around and go back. There was only one thing she could do. Leaving the food packet with him, she put on her shoes and started to walk.

———— ♥ ————

Sipho was tired. He had been away nearly a week and the cattle were not easy to control. The heat and dust did not make him feel any better. They needed rain badly. He was glad when they came to the farm 'Outspan' at last. When the last cow had been chased into the kraal and the gates closed, Sipho went to make a fire and prepare for a good night's rest. The two herdboys had been invited to spend the night with the farm workers but Sipho wanted to be alone. He was glad that old Kanczane had remembered to deliver the grain. That was one worry less. It was not yet dark but he wanted to start the fire and sleep early. He collected a few twigs and put them together, stuffing dry grass under them. He lit the fire, blew gently to start the small flames licking the dry wood when he suddenly felt he was not alone. When he looked up, nobody was there. Had he been wrong? He looked around but could see nothing. He shrugged. He was tired and his mind was playing tricks. He filled his cooking pot with water and was about to put it over the fire, when a hand came down on his.

'I'll do that.'

He looked up sharply and nearly dropped the pot. Tombi gave her wide, happy smile. 'I knew you would be tired and lonely. I've come to keep you company.'

Sipho stared at her. She wore very little in the heat that still hung in the air. 'Aren't you happy to see me?' Her thick lips pouted and she rolled her eyes at him. 'See . . . I'll even cook your food.'

Sipho was angry. Not at her, but because he was pleased to see her. When he shook his head at her and laughed, she knew the rest would be easy.

22

Double Betrayal

Nomsa was worried. 'He won't be happy to see her,' she said to Petrus as the donkey cart went off down the road.

'Maybe not,' Petrus agreed. 'But if the spirits of our fathers have tied the cord tight enough around their love, they will know.'

Great was their surprise when, nearly two hours later, Lindi came running into the house. She was out of breath and covered with dust, sweating freely from the heat of the midday sun. 'Tombi lied!' she shouted. 'She lied to me! I know where Sipho is! I have to go . . . now! There isn't much time left!'

Nomsa and Petrus stared at her. 'Go? Go where?'

'To Sipho! Baba . . . I must take Betta! I must! It's all I have. If I walk, I won't get there in time!'

'In time for what?' Nomsa did not understand her wild, angry daughter.

'To stop Tombi telling more lies about me! She hates me and loves Sipho! She wants him for herself and will do anything to get him!'

Her parents looked at each other then at Lindi. 'But the mule is old and half blind, Lindidwe!' Nomsa cried.

'She knows me, Mama . . . she'll get me there, even if I must walk part of the way.'

Upset, worried and afraid, Petrus and Nomsa clung to each other and let her go.

———— ♥ ————

Sipho kicked out the fire and stood up. 'Come,' he said gruffly. 'I'll make a bed for you in the feed room behind the kraal. There is lots of grass and you can take my blanket.'

'Where will you sleep?' Tombi looked at him through her lashes and pulled her skirt up her legs as she kneeled to collect the cooking pots and spoons. She knew he was looking at her.

Sipho coughed and cleared his throat. 'Don't worry, you'll be safe. I won't be far away.'

Tombi said nothing. She had been very good and not said or done anything to make him cross or upset. She knew he would do the proper thing by giving her his blanket while he slept in the truck. Because of this, she knew what she would do. Later. When the time was right.

After Sipho had made Tombi comfortable, he walked out into the starlit night. The moon hung in the sky like a slice of yellow cheese, throwing little light over the dark, ghostly shapes around him. He went to his truck and pulled out a thick coat he kept behind the seat. He was a big man and the cab of the truck was small. He would not get much sleep that night.

An hour later he heard her scream. He had been half asleep and was not sure whether it had not been a calf crying for its mother. He sat up and listened. When she screamed again, he threw open the door and ran to the kraal, his long coat flapping around his heels. When at last he opened the feed room door, Tombi threw herself at him.

'Snake!' she screamed and tightened her arms around his neck. 'It went over me!'

Sipho tried to unwind her arms. He could hardly breathe, but she would not let go. She pushed her face into his neck, pressing herself against him. 'Don't leave me or I'll die! Stay with me! I'm terribly frightened . . .!'

Sipho tried to step back. 'If there's a snake I must find it,' he said, but Tombi held him even tighter.

'No . . . it's gone now. Sipho! You can't leave me now!' She pretended to cry and started kissing him, her full wet lips on his face . . . his neck . . . his chest. When she pulled him down to the grass, he groaned. Tombi had won at last.

———————— ♥ ————————

Lindi wanted to cry. Betta would not move a step more. She lay with her belly hard against the dust and blinked at Lindi with her sad, half-blind eyes.

'We're so very close now, Betta . . . please . . . you must get up!' She pushed and pulled but it was no good. Betta would not get up. Lindi knew she would have to walk the rest of the way. But what to do about the mule? She could not leave her lying on the road. She remembered passing a herd of goats and a small boy looking after them. It was her only hope. The boy agreed to take Betta home with the goats and look after her until Lindi got back.

Halfway down the road Lindi looked at the sky. Another hour and it would be dark. She would never make it to 'Outspan' in time. There was no moon and it would be impossible to look for Sipho in the dark. Her legs felt weak and heavy and her feet were sore with broken blisters. Across the field, she saw a light flicker from a small farmhouse. There was nothing she could do except ask for shelter for the night. She took off her shoes and limped slowly across the field to wait for the dawn.

———————— ♥ ————————

At daybreak, Sipho woke up and felt Tombi's heavy body against his. She was still sleeping, her head resting on her hand. Bits of grass stuck in her stiff dark hair and she was snoring softly. Sipho rolled away, ashamed and disgusted. He blamed himself for he could not blame her. Everybody knew that Tombi gave her body away easily because she was man mad. He should have been strong. He tried to get up without waking her but she moved closer and threw her arm around his chest. When he pulled away she woke up and started to kiss him, moaning and grunting with pleasure. He tried to push her away, his hands on her shoulders when the door suddenly opened. The fresh, cool light of dawn spilled through like a spotlight and fell on them. Sipho covered his face with his hands and gave a low cry like an animal in pain. In that moment his life shattered into a million pieces before the sight of Lindi standing in the doorway.

———— ♥ ————

Lindi had left the farmer's small house while it was still dark. They had welcomed her kindly. The farmer's wife had bathed her sore feet and fed her hot soup and home-baked bread. But she could not sleep and an hour before dawn, she was on her way to 'Outspan' and – Sipho.

'The big man with the beard and the lame leg? Yes, he is camping over there by the kraal near the dam . . .' The little herdboy looked at Lindi in surprise, his eyes still dull with sleep. She had come like a ghost out of the grey dawn and found him sleeping in a sheep kraal, his skinny yellow dog at his side.

Lindi thanked the boy and hurried to the cattle kraal next to the dam. Her heart was beating very fast and her mouth was dry. Half running, half limping, she came to the kraal and saw the feed room on the side of it. He had to be inside.

Without knocking or wasting another moment, she flung open the door. Nothing was real. It could not be. She was tired and in pain. Her mind was playing devilish tricks on her. She shook her head as if to clear a mist before her eyes but the evil picture would not go away. She lifted her hands to her face and stepped back, shaking her head from side to side, desperately wanting to clear the sight of Sipho and Tombi together. When it did not go away, she gave a terrible cry and rushed in, throwing herself at Tombi.

'You filthy . . . dirty . . . low born slut! I'll kill you for this!' she screamed and struck Tombi on the head. She slapped her face and pulled her ears and hair. 'You're nothing but a liar . . . a cheat . . .' With every insult, Lindi slapped Tombi hard across her face, kneeling over her and panting like a half crazed animal. Tombi screamed and tried to fight back but Lindi's anger gave her unnatural strength. It was happening so quickly and had come so suddenly that Sipho did not know what to do. It was only when Lindi tore her nails across Tombi's bare flesh and drew blood, that he grabbed her arms. Tombi's shrill screams blotted out his cry for Lindi to stop. But Lindi heard nothing . . . saw nothing but the red hot mist of hate for the girl she was attacking. He had never seen her this way. She had been gone all this time and now to come together like this!

He would gladly have let Lindi kill him in Tombi's place but he knew he could not sit back and do nothing to save the girl from Lindi's terrible anger.

'Lindi stop! Stop it!' He tried to twist her arms behind her, pulling her off Tombi at the same time. He held Lindi tightly against him and tried to calm her. She was shaking and sobbing violently, kicking and struggling, trying to bite his hands – anything to free herself from his iron hard grip.

'You let me go! You are just as bad as her! How could you lie with such dirt! How could you! How could you! I thought you loved me! I thought you . . . loved . . . me!' It was too much for Lindi and she broke down. All the fight went out of her and she fell like a rag doll in Sipho's arms, crying bitterly. He tried to comfort her but at the sound of his voice, she lashed out. 'Don't come near me! Don't . . . ever . . . come near me again! Do you hear?' She ran to the door and pointed a shaking finger at Tombi. 'Take her! She's always wanted you! So take her and I hope . . . I hope you both rot.'

She gave Sipho a wild look of hate mixed with hurt, disappointment and anger. Then she looked at Tombi and spat before she turned and ran from the kraal as fast as her burning, blistered feet could take her.

23

Two Hearts Beat as One

Lindi sat under a thorn tree and cried. She thought Sipho would follow her but he did not. The pain of seeing Sipho with Tombi and the fiery pain of her feet was like burning alive. She wanted to die. With Sipho out of her life she had nothing to live for. She could not believe his love for Tombi was greater than his love for her. She tried to blame him – hate him even, but deep in her heart she knew that she was the one to blame. She had been away too long. Sipho had heard nothing from her. How could she now blame him for giving in to Tombi's trickery when she was more guilty than he was?

Her loud cries of shame and self-pity were soon heard by the herdboy's yellow dog who started barking. She was very glad to see the herdboy who looked at her with big round eyes. 'My feet are too sore to walk,' she sniffed. 'Can you get somebody to help me?'

She waited nearly half an hour before she heard somebody coming back. 'I'm here,' she called. 'Boy? Is that you?' A twig snapped behind her and she turned quickly. The boy and his dog were nowhere to be seen but – 'You!'

She tried to stand up but cried out in pain. Sipho caught her as she fell. She tried to get away from him but as she twisted her head sharply to one side, his hand came down hard over her mouth. 'If you act like a wildcat then I must treat you as one,' he said gruffly. 'Will you stay still and let me help you or must I leave you for the crows to peck out your eyes?' He was not trying to be funny. His voice was as cold and hard as his arms around her. She stopped struggling and sank to the ground. Sipho looked at her feet. 'I'll take you to the house,' he said. 'The old lady will help you.'

Without waiting for her reply, he picked her up and carried her to his truck. Lindi could do nothing but accept his help. She lay quietly in his arms, neither of them speaking a word. Nor did he say anything when he left her later with the farmer's wife. She wanted to thank him but saw he had already limped away, his back stiff and straight, his head high. She could not help wondering whether he was going back to Tombi. Hot tears of hurt and heartache filled her eyes and slid down her cheeks. The old lady saw them and gently took her hand. 'Shame, child . . . don't cry. I've got just the right *imuti* to make your feet good as new. Shhh now, don't cry . . .' But her kindness only made Lindi's tears flow faster as she was led into the comfort of the farmhouse kitchen.

———— ♥ ————

After Sipho had chased Tombi out of his life with the threat of killing her if she ever came near him again, his sorrow at being caught with Tombi all at once changed to anger. He blamed Lindi bitterly for everything that had happened. She had caught him trapped in a lie with a girl he hated – but was Lindidwe not as guilty? She had found a rich handsome boy in the city. What gave her the right to stand and blame him for being unfaithful? With these bitter thoughts poisoning his love for her, he decided once and for all to put her out of his mind and try to forget her. He did not know that at that very same moment, Lindi was blaming herself just as much and that she would never stop blaming herself until the day Sipho again spoke her name with love and forgiveness.

———— ♥ ————

Old Granny looked at Lindi through the fringe of beaded wildebeest hair hanging over her eyes. They had spent two long hours together and now the *sangoma* knew everything.

'What must I do, Old Granny?' Lindi hung her head and

spoke in a whisper. 'I am more sorry than I have been about anything in my life.'

'There is no power greater than love,' the old woman said. 'You must do as your heart tells you. If Sipho loves you he will listen and in the end fire will melt ice. Go to him.'

She dug around inside her skin bag. 'Here . . . take this. Keep it with you always. When you carry Sipho's child, bring it back to me.'

Later, halfway down the hill, Lindi sat on a rock and looked at the charm. She pressed it to her lips and then to her heart. She would make sure she had it with her always and at night she would sleep with it under her pillow. More than her life, she wanted Sipho's love back. If she failed, she would have nothing left except a broken heart and a future without hope.

It took Lindi over a week before the charm gave her the courage to go to Sipho. She had not seen him since the day he had left her at 'Outspan' – nearly a month ago. If he was not away from Kwamakutha, he was always working.

Lindi could not eat or sleep properly. She had to speak to Sipho. She could not wait a day longer. As always, he was not alone on the day she found him at the cattle kraal. His long-horned cows were being dipped against tick-borne fever and he was supervising the work. One by one the beasts were herded through a narrow gate and, bellowing loudly, fell into the deep water tank. Lindi watched them swim through the milky water and scramble up the other side where they stood dripping in the sun. Sipho did not stop when he saw her. Taking no notice of the noise of cattle cries and the shouting, whistling and cursing of the herd boys, he asked her what she wanted.

'What? Speak louder! I can't hear you!' he shouted and pushed the heel of his boot hard against a cow's side, sliding her into the tank with a splash that wet Lindi's dress. She jumped back and swallowed the ache in her throat.

'I said I've come to thank you . . .' she began, but Sipho

127

turned his head and shouted an order to the herd boy at the far end of the dipping tank. Lindi's eyes burned with tears. He did not care whether she was there or not. If she had been one of his precious cows drowning in the tank, he would have cared more. She turned and walked away, pain spreading like a red hot flame inside her chest.

She had not gone far when Sipho came up behind her and grabbed her arm. 'Wait!'

She stopped and looked at him. He was dirty and wet and smelled of cattle dip and sweat – and she loved him. She loved him so much at that moment that it was only the icy look in his dark eyes that stopped her from throwing herself into his arms. She wanted to cry away all the pain and bitterness that was between them and stop the torture that was tearing their love apart.

'You said something I didn't hear,' he said, his hand still on her arm.

Lindi blinked back her tears. 'I wanted to thank you for helping me last month.'

Sipho looked disappointed. 'Is that all? I would have done the same for a wounded goat. It was nothing.' He dropped her arm and was about to go when she called him.

'Sipho? I . . . I just want to say how sorry I am . . .'

But Sipho turned and limped away saying something she did not hear. Lindi ran up to him and this time it was she who took hold of his arm. 'Sipho please . . . we have to talk. There is so much . . .'

'So much what, Lindidwe?' he broke in harshly. 'So much to tell me about the good time you had in the city? So much about the wonderful man you lived with? I saw the letter from your aunt! One letter . . . but not from you!'

'I can explain . . . please listen to me . . .'

'No! You listen to me!' Sipho gripped her elbow. 'You're right. Maybe we should talk but not here.' He almost lifted her from the ground as he took her to a nearby barn. It was cool and quiet inside. He pushed her in and closed the wooden door, sliding the bolt closed.

'There was a man in Bethsada wasn't there?' He glared at her. 'Is that why you didn't write?'

Lindi's hands balled into fists at her side.

'Yes . . . no . . .'

'So! It's true!'

His anger was like fire feeding fire and she felt her own blood run hot.

'And what about you?' she shouted. 'It didn't take you long to find your pleasure in Tombi's arms!'

'Tombi?' Sipho looked surprised. 'What has she to do with this?'

'Everything! I saw you! You and that . . . that cow!'

She could not believe it when Sipho threw back his head and laughed. 'Tombi? I would rather bed with a snake than her!' Sipho did not go on. How could he forget the one and only time his weak flesh had failed him? As had Lindidwe's and he told her so. She stared at him, hurt and guilty but when he shouted, 'Why did you come home, Lindidwe? To show me how much better a man he is than I . . .' she slapped him hard across his face.

'Stop it!' She tried to hit him again but he caught her raised hand and pulled her hard against him, his beard scraping her face.

'Why Lindidwe? Does the truth sting like a scorpion's tail?' His eyes were black with anger and his breath hot on her cheek.

'Let me go!' She struggled and fought him with all her strength. When he did not listen, she nipped his ear with her teeth.

Cursing, Sipho flung her from him. She lost her balance and fell back on to a pile of loose hay. 'I hate you Sipho Sosibo!' she cried and tried to get up. 'I hate you! Go to your Tombi . . . I don't care! I don't care any more, do you hear? I never want to . . .' But Sipho stopped her angry words by falling next to her and crushing his mouth down on hers. He rolled over her and held her fast while she kicked and screamed and struggled to get free.

Suddenly Sipho's longing and desire during the empty, waiting weeks without her flamed into a passionate hunger. All his anger, hate, despair and the cruel thoughts of her with another man melted into a love greater than anything else. When at last Lindi stopped struggling and began to moan and whisper his name with as much passion as his own, he knew that the wasted, misunderstood weeks of pain and suffering were over. Nothing would ever come between them again. Sipho was going to make quite sure of that.

———— ♥ ————

'So . . . it has happened?' Old Granny gave Lindi a wide, toothless smile.

Lindi nodded. She held out the charm the *sangoma* had given her so long ago, it now seemed. 'Then he has forgiven you? Every evil thing that happened in the city is now washed clean between you?'

Lindi shook her head. 'I wanted to wash everything clean, Old Granny, but he wouldn't listen. He said that the time of darkness was over and we must look only to the light. It was then that our child was conceived. A sign that we would never again be separated from each other.'

Old Granny nodded. 'And the girl? Tombi?'

'She has gone to live with her grandparents in the valley otherside Kwamakutha. She will not trouble us . . . especially now.'

'Because you are carrying his child?'

'Yes . . . Sipho's child – perhaps a son.'

The *sangoma's* belly shook with silent laughter. 'What else but a son would spring from the loins of a man such as Sipho Sosibo?'

'Then you will give the child your blessing on the day it is born?'

'As I will on the day of your wedding feast, child.' Old Granny clapped her dry, bony hands together, her feet shuffling the dust in a mock dance. With the *sangoma's* song following her down the hill, Lindi went to find her Sipho.

———— ♥ ————

In the dying heat of late summer, they sat together under the willow trees by the river. Very gently, Sipho put his hand on the soft round swelling of her belly and felt the baby kick. He laughed and pulled his beloved Lindi against his chest.

'It's a fine little bull I have sired, *sthandwa!*'

'And if it's a girl? Will you still marry me?' She pretended to pull away, her small fists against his chest.

'Boy or girl, it will be our child. What do you think? Will I slaughter a bull . . . make music . . . get drunk and feast on my wedding night without a wife to suckle my child?'

'Sipho!' Lindi pulled his beard and her laughter was like the water that rippled over the river rocks and flooded his heart with joy.

As the late afternoon sun slipped behind the hills of Kwamakutha in a blaze of red and gold, they heard the sound of a distant African drum.

'Listen . . . it's coming on the wind . . .'

He nodded and drew her close. 'The spirits of our fathers are giving us their blessing, *sthandwa*.'

Side by side, in the growing dusk, they sat and listened. Then slowly and silently the wind died down until they heard only their heartbeats against the sound of the river that like their love, would flow on forever.

131

HEINEMANN HEARTBEATS

The book you have been reading is part of the new
Heinemann Heartbeats series. Details of some of the other
titles available are listed below.

❤

A Bride for the King
NANDI DLOVU

Beautiful Zible dearly loves Saul. Then the royal *sangoma* declares
that Zible will marry Saul's half-brother – the king. The young
lovers are heart-broken. Against a background of sorcery and
intrigue, Zible prepares to meet her fate . . .

❤

Stolen Kisses
MICHELLE MWANSA

Shy schoolgirl Patience meets young lawyer Artwell Nkosi in the
library. She is swept off her feet. Is this true love, or is Artwell
really after her sister, the glamorous model Thandiwe?

❤

The Gift of Life
PATRICIA CAGE

When Thembi wins the heart of Mduduzi, everyone agrees that
this is a match made in heaven. Suddenly, at their engagement
party, disaster strikes. Will things ever be the same again?

❤

Please Forgive Me
ROSINA UMELO

Oke and Bukky love each other dearly. But Oke's sister, Udoka, will have nothing to do with the girlfriend she calls a witch. Oke and Udoka are involved in a tragic car accident and suddenly it all looks like Bukky's fault . . .

———— ♥ ————

Heart of Love
HOPE DUBE

Claudette is hard-working and new to the company. She is bright and beautiful. Charles Daka is her boss, and is rich, successful and single. How can Claudette get him to take her seriously and find her attractive?

———— ♥ ————

Love Changes Everything
KALU OKPI

In exile in Nigeria, stylish Gavinah finds love in the arms of Onyeukwu, law student and rock musician. But her tragic past soon catches up with her and it seems that the young lovers will never be together . . .

———— ♥ ————

The Jasmine Candle
CHRISTINE A. BOTCHWAY

Zenobia, a mysterious beauty, lives a lonely life in a land between two ancient tribes. Even her childhood friend Odole doesn't want to know her. Then she breaks a taboo and Odole is ordered to kill her. Our heroine seems doomed.

———— ♥ ————

Love Snare
JAMES IRUNGU

Sweet, innocent Emma is excited when she lands an important new job. She hasn't bargained for her new manager – the ruthless playboy J. N. Mwea. Mwea's old flame wants to capture him again. Emma's very life is soon in danger.

———— ♥ ————

The Place of Gentle Waters
JESSICA MAJI

Scientist Anne Caldwell arrives from Britain to go to Richard Giba's Kenyan farm to help him with a problem. She soon finds herself attracted to him. But Anne has a dark secret . . .

———— ♥ ————